Blue Field

BLUE FIELD

ELISE LEVINE

A JOHN METCALF BOOK

BIBLIOASIS
WINDSOR, ONTARIO

FIRST EDITION

Library and Archives Canada Cataloguing in Publication

Levine, Elise, author

    Blue field / Elise Levine.

Issued in print and electronic formats.

ISBN 978-1-77196-151-6 (softcover).--ISBN 978-1-77196-152-3 (ebook)

    I. Title.

PS8573.E9647B58 2017   C813'.54   C2016-907954-6

                                               C2016-907955-4

Readied for the press by John Metcalf
Copy-edited by Emily Donaldson
Typeset by Chris Andrechek
Cover designed by David Drummond

Canada Council Conseil des Arts
for the Arts du Canada

ONTARIO ARTS COUNCIL
CONSEIL DES ARTS DE L'ONTARIO
50 YEARS OF ONTARIO GOVERNMENT SUPPORT OF THE ARTS
50 ANS DE SOUTIEN DU GOUVERNEMENT DE L'ONTARIO AUX ARTS

Canadian Patrimoine
Heritage canadien

Published with the generous assistance of the Canada Council for the Arts and the Ontario Arts Council. Biblioasis also acknowledges the support of the Government of Canada through the Canada Book Fund and the Government of Ontario through the Ontario Book Publishing Tax Credit.

PRINTED AND BOUND IN CANADA

For D

Do not mourn the dead. They know what they are doing.
—Clarice Lispector (trans. Benjamin Moser)

PART ONE

1

She hung. Fifty feet beneath the high-noon surface, over glinting beer cans and pouting bass, her breath-exhaust balled upward like starburst—and when her shadow in his black suit and hood bumped her, she tumbled as if through sky. Memory-flash of song, mildew scent of old-dog fur, whoosh down white fathoms. His gloved hand clamped her shoulder and he pressed his mask to hers. Cratered skin floodlit, beard-stubble blue. Eyes flushed. Weeping? She could hardly believe. His other hand hove into view and jiggered the regulator in her mouth. She clenched her jaw and snorted. Fuck. Could he be more in her face?

All she was also pissed at—death of her parents, cancer and a subway bomb within days of each other, boom-boom then a comet tail of grief sparking in their wake, year of parched, thirsty. The recent succession of colourful drinks like cheerleaders' pompons. An expensive, complicated hair cut. Work and more work and colourless classes her closest friend urged. Lives of the Post-Poets. Meditate-Don't-Medicate Your Mood. A medical-textbook illustrator who'd never helped anyone she knew personally, when she bit her tongue the blood ran grey—until the Learn to Dive course. Once a week she crouched rabid as a harpy mermaid on the pool floor and found the turquoise underworld stowed her. Protests and non-mandated ordinations and tail-spin economies dangled here like glinting spinners she refused. She hunkered in and held her breath despite the instructor's fog-horned edicts warning of pulmonary embolism. Inky black scrolled through her vision. Behind its scrim she grew a new heart, green—strange new creature worthy of further inquiry, she thought, emboldened by the chlorine ethers, the weightlessness. So she performed drill upon drill and nailed her certification test and, curious enough to bite again, promptly proposed to the dive master. Open-water date?

Suck-bang—his respirations, hers. A pneumatic storm. Suspension of teal fish. He shook his big head after a moment—you win—and let her go, then rolled into ribbons of eelgrass and disappeared. She lazed again among zebra-striped dorsals, ogled canker-lipped perch. Floating particulate glimmered. Suddenly he came at her from above, enormous as an airship. He locked onto her with a shudder and ferried her to the lakebed where she sank in the marl. Where on earth were her legs and arms? Mud spirited away much of her sight. She struggled, goggles knocked. Cold liquid slicked in and a pin pricked open inside her. Gone—mother handing her a small ancient package bandaged white. Pain parcel. Gone the smell of urine and candy, chemo's whiteout. Selling childhood's backyard sparrows, old tree with its branches like busted brains. Girl-junk milky and sour. Poof, bottom's up, cheers.

She let him have it. Spat out her reg and reared her neck back and hissed the air from her lungs. The muck semi-parted and she got her index finger up and crooked it. What the? He removed his own reg and sealed her lips with his. His tongue twisting hers made another question mark. He withdrew and popped her mouthpiece back into place. She gritted her teeth on the silicone, hacked out her lung's last withheld nugget, drew in fresh breath. Surprised she still could. Surprised by her surprise. And by *his* bent, black-gloved finger. Well?

2

They checked into a motel room and ripped it for real. After—sticky, cooling—they lay side by side on the floor. Yeah, she drawled. Double that, he said.

Late October, late afternoon. Blue leaked onto the walls from where the curtains refused to fully close. Bruised sheets and carpet—even skin was a blue echo. They rose and shook out their limbs. As if blue were the colour of starving, they foraged the shabby corridor's vending machine, scarfed candy bars and chips. They made love again, crinkling amid foil wrappers. When it was over she tucked the bedcover beneath her chin. So anyway, she said. What's your story? Where'd you come from?

He nuzzled his long strange feet against hers. She'd already stolen moments to peruse the pale second toes nearly double the length of his big ones. Now she imagined prodding and prising the elongated proximal phalanxes with her mechanical pencil, imagined her own renewed interest in modelling body parts with her soft-wares. But he just stuffed his hands beneath his head and pursed his lips. Pitted scars on his face and chest suggested volcanic kid-acne. Who, what hatched him? Story short, he said. I was adopted, grew up happy, the end.

She recalled her mother sporting a happy birthday hat, sundress straps askew. Father's eyeglasses bristling with reflected cake-candles. She nudged around for the recently familiar feelings—anger, ashes—and drew a blank on which the morning's wavy motion of the water soon teetered. She gripped the edge of the mattress with one hand. Funny, she managed to say. I'm kind of an orphan as well.

He dislodged the cover and nudged her to his side. You okay? he asked, a blued sweat pooling in tender droplets on his temples.

Soon he was crusty where his penis drowsed against her belly. She got up to pee, flushed. She splashed water in the sink and drew the bathroom curtains apart. Night now. Lit by a single streetlamp, fog foundered in the motel parking lot amid drifts of leaves. She shivered. Pressure in her ears. A drop formed on the faucet and hung like a sac. From the bed, an impatient mattress creak.

Too soon again they packed into his truck and rode out beneath an overcast dawn strung with trances of migrating geese. An hour of dun fields and he pulled over. They were miles still from the nearest checkpoints. Wind gasped pebbles at the truck's undercarriage and razzed the windshield. He roughed his stubble with his thick-jointed fingers and a predatory beat invaded her head—water-borne bacteria scaling her canals and tympanum, who knew? Infection and appointments and permanent hearing loss.

Stay with me tonight? he said.

Can't. Early meetings tomorrow.

He knocked the truck back into gear. Right, he said. I get it. Too far, too fast.

Not what I meant, she said, mind skidding toward tomorrow's mirror-skinned towers and similitudes of corridors and parking lots, the nodding and rictus-smiling as she laid out her wares. And then the rush-hour armadas of oncoming headlights, possible curbside immolations backdropped by six-story digi-boards promising the latest administration's RenewalWorks! campaign. All this near-life she'd been ungrateful for since her parents' deaths.

But once upon a time—the summer she was fourteen—time had stood still. She'd followed her best friend in breaching a newly discovered gap in the chain-link fence behind the convenience store and descended a honeysuckle dripping, thorny realm to a hidden creek forbidden throughout their childhoods. She and her friend returned daily but what was a day then? Cicada-time, girl-time of cigarettes filched from parents turned statues by coursing girl-hormones, of hash brownies and baked-baby brownies and other sundry legends. Wild dominion of fast friends who traced freckles on each other's backs and told fortunes that turned into toads or jumped ship hands clasped and never let go. Glorious escape and then no escape when, just before school started that fall, Works! Workers razed and landfilled the ravine for BestBet Towers soon ringed by SureBets and SafeBets.

In the truck beside her, her date stage-coughed. Verdict still out? he prompted. There hope for me yet?

Early-season flakes melted through the gusts outside. She laughed and squeezed her eyes shut. Retinal noise lit up behind her closed lids. Floaters and fireworks, her optic apparatus peacocking, she knew. But still. She opened her eyes again. The urgent stare on him. And that blue oddly still at his temples. Charmer, she said.

He shipped to attention then lashed back against the seat. He raised both hands high as if under arrest.

3

A third consecutive morning she woke freezing in his bed. Her new normal. He was turned away with his face buried in one of the king pillows. A miracle he wasn't suffocating. Rain frosted the tall windows in his upper-floor suite. She wrapped herself around his warmth as if he might tug her to wherever he was afloat in his own slack unconscious, one that ran at a higher temperature than hers. Water ticked from the tap in the next-door bathroom. She pressed her nose harder to his back, eliciting a grunt. The best response, she decided, to her handset's unreturned messages from her friend—where r u? u alright?—ghosting on the bedside table. Because how account? At least she'd dragged through most of her work these past days—as had he, for that matter. No harm done. No harm! And if she got up soon and got dressed and to her apartment on the district's far side, plunked at her desk and last-gasped through her latest project, she'd crank it out on time. She would.

Or else. Still, she touched him now above his buttocks and along his outer thighs. He mumbled awake, turned onto his back and lifted the sheet for her to mount him.

An ugly man. Raw-knuckled, raggedy-nailed. Accretions of muscles on his torso like carbuncles on a powerful creature's hide. That blue by his temples now an efflorescence like pin-dot schools of fish. Here and not here. Here, over here. Come here.

He sweated salt. His short hair quilled like a crown.

Enough with the pissing and moaning. She waggled aboard. Shadows flowed from the walls. She worked out how to arch her brittle-star spine and bloom algae between her thighs. Her ribcage a lyre. Strum-strum, strum-strum. What she'd confess to, and what she wouldn't, was no matter. No matter at all.

4

For the first time in over a week she poked her car through the cemetery's entrance. *Pardes Shalom*, peaceful garden. Up the rise the granite rows winked against the sun. She cut the engine and got out. She'd run late all morning—sex, meetings, traffic by the crap-ton— but here everything seemed suspended in the freak heat haze. She tucked her damp dress between her thighs and knelt at the Y-joint of the paved path—a left into a hedge-rimmed distance, a right along the scalloped edges of sprinklered turf—and when she clawed inside the steel bucket, quartz dust rose like steam. She stood and sneezed. Dizzy, panting. The stones glittered in her palm and her fingers itched. Days ago there'd been sleet and hail. Though admittedly she'd hardly noticed much of anything aside from her sudden preoccupation, with its nearly assassinating private pleasures. But now, here, the white sky boiled. The Scotch pines were like green flames.

She rubbed her eyes. They felt like grit in her face.

She spiked her heels up the incline then stopped part way and scuffled off her tight shoes. Underfoot, a spongy hint of cool. If only she weren't stuck topside, AC-less and bereft and scorched at the clavicle, nipples seared. Ridiculous at noon. Mom? Dad? Her throat smoked and hoarsened. She imagined swallowing swords. Hunched like a shrinking sideshow attraction—de-salinizing, feeling every inch of her twenty-nine years going on ninety-nine—she resumed huffing the hill, one of a series of concentric waves stretching to the east and ending in a diminutive red-pine forest. Beyond the cemetery's carefully cultivated repose—pricey, for certain, though her parents had thoughtfully shelled a bundle twenty years previous, and then worried loudly ever since about their rapidly diminishing investments—lay hundreds if not thousands of developments serpentining in linked byways and then chopped into inscrutably isolated parcels. Townhouse and compound and browning golf course. Strip mall and mall brightened by glorious, invasive ground cover. She pictured never finding her way back home. Better off tramping here forever, forever shielding her eyes with a hand and searching for her parents' marker but never making it out. Never arriving, as if she were hauling rope and more rope, nothing but ever-growing rope.

She tramped on. How could she have forgotten? If she let go, she'd have nothing but nothing.

She tottered atop the ridge and located the headstone. Soon she was scrabbling room for her latest offerings on its broad shelf. Rock and more rock. A dry trail resembling the desiccated tear-pellets a heartless giant might once have shed. The sun blazed higher. But a transmission of warm wind lifted her dank hair, and a good cry brought proof—despite her missed visits, she was here. Still here. Her parents too. It was as if they'd fallen down a long well and hadn't managed to clamber free. She stopped crying and ran her hands over her bare arms to feel her follicles, alert as antennae.

Back in the car she smoothed her dress, extracted a tissue from the glove box and spat, swabbed the scurf from her lashes. She got the AC blasting and peered through the windshield. Birds still blotted holes in the sky and whistled their old tunes. Beyond, in the smog-horizon, a rainbow smut. She lingered, admiring the view. High above where the sky appeared a clearest blue, tiny bright dots sparked and jiggled—her own white blood cells bounding through the narrows of her retina's blood vessels. The blue-field optical phenomenon. It looked like a screen across her perceptual field. For a second the dots above her car gathered blizzard force and she felt herself lift and toggle as if among them.

She remembered true winter here. The cruel wind flurrying a relentless snow. The watcher who in accordance with ancient custom attended her mother's casket atop the hill while she the dutiful daughter collected her father from the car and drew him up the path to the gravesite. All the while the *shomer* waited, guarding the body but watching her, she felt, judging, a feeling she couldn't shake. And once there, Jesus! her father called out. The rabbi startled, then rolled—*Baruch* this, *Adonai* that, what a pro. Soon her father looked like he was boiling, curses bubbling into the December air. She surreptitiously looked around—the watcher had melted away—and twice she tried to take her father by the arm, get him to settle, maybe coax him along the shovelled path and put him in the car and lock the door on him. But no go. Each time she plucked the sleeve of his old duffel jacket he shook free, swore like a stevedore, some of which tribe he'd once known personally as general manager of a shipping company, contending with lay-offs, strikes, Ukrainian stowaways, the city in those days still a major port.

Jesus! all through Kaddish. She stiffened in her parka and occasionally flicked a drop or two from her face. Nearby a stick-thin distant cousin shivered in a tiny black wrap, ungloriously underdressed for a Hanukkah burial—Jesus. Hard to believe. Apparently the cousin's only dress coat was red and apparently not even she had the nerve to pull that off. At least the freaking cold was working in favour of the parka, since beneath it was a pantsuit that used to fit but was now tighter than drying rope. Earlier that morning she'd dressed in her just-deceased-mother's disorderly bathroom. Dizzied by thoughts of what to keep, what toss—useless for her final journey the dull manicure scissors, eye cream, four nearly finished jars of Vaseline, what the fuck?—she'd handled her belly fat then sucked it in and yanked the zipper, tortured in private places. But with the funeral underway she was thinking the cold could be even colder.

She imagined a rent-lung clarity. A vacuum-packed nothing. Freedom through freeze-drying. Rebirth as astronaut-drift in an unblinking beyond. Escape! Instead there was the snow—was it ever coming down, fogging the surrounding hills. Leaving not much to look at except the hole in the ground and the lilac-coloured coffin, dainty, impractical—pre-selected by Mom herself—and about to be wholly surrendered while the living blinked, unfathoming. They were fudged, smuzzy. Something they hadn't seemed before. For one thing they were in a section of the cemetery reserved for the deceased of a local Labour Zionist congregation. Her father, who hadn't attended a service since the cousin's bat mitzvah and certainly counted himself as no member of any group, had purchased the double plot here because it was by far the cheapest available, in his books a moral victory of sorts. Making small talk with the rabbi pre-service, good old Dad had make-believed about so-and-sos there was no way he knew, holy days he'd last celebrated in the Antediluvian Era. When the rabbi asked how many years husband and wife had shared, the answer was a fantasy beast of fifty of the best creation had ever bestowed. A creature called Dummy, she immediately thought—what her father used to call her mother when, during their frequent fights, he broke a lot of furniture trying to break his spouse's warrior silence. Hearing such lies, who wouldn't want to call such a father out? Who wouldn't re-tighten her thick scarf and fume instead? Of all times. Of all places.

But when the rabbi finished reciting, her father totally lost it. Jesus, he shouted, tears streaming his cheeks. Jesus.

She steadied her gaze on the shovels spiked like spears in the hard dirt heaped around the grave's perimeter.

There was scaffolding too and wide straps, some kind of gizmo for lowering the box and conducting the business at hand. She kept her back turned on pretty much everything else—she'd already seen her cousin managing, despite her shaking and quaking, to leaf her hands through her thick hair. No friends. No people her mother had never cared much for. She'd been embarrassed to have lung cancer. Years of smoking, what she'd openly referred to as her filthy habit, had finally caught up to her. When she'd received her diagnosis, how hard it had been to convince her not to say she had breast cancer instead—she thought it might gain her greater sympathy, pink ribbons, stuffed toys, balloons. Some prize. How much she must have lived confused in her head. Whose own head wouldn't swim just thinking? Whose legs wouldn't wobble?

So when her father began racing the wooden plank alongside the grave, backing and forthing over the now-descending casket, its cargo of emaciated body wrapped in a white sheet, she let him be.

The purity of that sheet had been important, evidently. Keeping it that way had caused some consternation. She'd driven in the middle of the night from her south-city-district apartment to arrive at her parents' bungalow crammed with a riot of meds and a ripe cat-litter box, her father exhausted and possibly incorrectly, dangerously drugged into brief acquiescence accepting coffee, a buttered roll—the bread not too far past its use-by date. By mid-morning came the phone call. This from some clown at the funeral home. There was a problem. In accordance with custom they'd wrapped her mother in a white sheet. But as sometimes happened with the dead, the guy explained, she was a cauldron inside, stomach acids and bile emitting a staining fluid at the mouth. Took a moment to comprehend. The only way to keep the sheet pure was to sew the lips shut. Permission was being sought. The old man, too out of it to deal, passed on the matter.

She clutched the phone to her ear. Why hesitate?

All those times she'd begged. Eat, please. Anything, especially toward the end. Mushy pasta with bottled, over-salted sauce. Simulac by the teaspoonful. In those last months, she'd desperately tried to ark as many calories as she could into her mother. Get her to pack some on. Get her to live. But her mother hadn't wanted any of it.

Yes, go right ahead, she told the funeral-home guy. Do what you need to do. Do it!

He seemed taken aback, stammering a few words before cutting short the call. But she hadn't cared. Here was some news. All along her mother had been full. On her surface, mute suffering, blankety-blank. Inside, a delicacy of churning eels. Lobster claws click-clacking—*tref*, impure, an unbridled unclean with which in death she was well-provisioned, leaving just some foam breach-burping her lips.

Please, the rabbi was saying. I'm afraid. Your father could fall.

Here was her teetering, imprecating father. Here the snow curling like the crests of waves over the leagues of the dead. So much for her magic carpet ride into the past. The rabbi shrugged apologetically and peered at his shoes. They were hefty numbers, scuffed, salt-soured. Clearly they'd seen better days. Like his face, the flesh listing, skin pouchy and pocked. Tell the distant cousin that, though. She'd sailed closer to the rabbi and cocked her hip, and was maneuvering her trembling bits and pieces in his direction. Now he looked really scared.

Jesus, Jesus.

She walked. She'd done it before, a lot. The second she'd turned eighteen—out of her parents' cramped house and into one squamous low-rent apartment after another. Whole emotional territories shipped and skipped, good riddance. Bullshit jobs tallying columns of numbers for questionable profits. Thieves for bosses. A degree then degrees then better jobs. Places to go, people to see. Including new young guys—the young dudes getting younger while she got on. So she went. But this time, toward what was left of her family—her riotous and undignified father—though the wooden board nearly bestride the grave was soaked and slippery. She inched toward him as he chuffed and capered and raged bare-headed—moments before, a flapping gust had disap-peared his yarmulke. When she got to him she gripped his arm. Jesus. How many times he'd gripped hers. She remembered it all, all of it, while Dad rocked on the plank and the rent-a-rabbi rolled and Mom's remains remained. Around them the tall pines waved their arms hello, good-bye—maybe in their language these were the same word. If she squinted, might the wet snow slip to apple blos-soms? At the rabbi's signal she opened her mouth. *Baruch Adonai.* Flakes lit her tongue. Flecks of cold-kissed stars, she thought, though she tried not to think. Hold on, she thought anyway—unsure of what she meant while amidst the bare trees, across the snow-swept swales, the winter sparrows dervished like dreidels. Like there was so much to cease to know.

Three days later, it was as if her father did topple in— as if in slow motion, his blown bits carefully collected by an organization she hired to place in a casket. So another watcher waited and watched until she stood before another rabbi and observed the casket lowering into the ground. The sky spun more snow, the flakes not much smaller than the small whirling birds. Who or what were any of them? The living, the dead. What was she to them? To anything? Hello, goodbye. *Baruch Adonai.* The stars were dead suns. Hold on.

After her father's graveside service she drove. God, did she. She'd hardly known who she was as she gripped her handset with one hand and steered with the other, scudding between ruts and potholes, past Regency Gardens and Buttermilk Estates, mind-trammeling apparitions of black ice. For some reason she couldn't understand, those past few days her best friend proved unreachable by any messaging device yet invented by humankind. But finally she got her fucking friend on the line.

For once their devices were getting brilliant reception. She felt stunned, confused, as if this were the real news. Shock, she supposed. Then she rasped her woes into the handset.

Oh god, her friend said. God, I'm so sorry.

And then the friend went off on her older sister before she could so much as get a sniffle in sideways. There was a Shehan involved. Or a Shawn. Or Sean. Cast of thousands. More confused, more stunned, but also brought back to the grace of easy complications, she offered a silent prayer of thanks. Her tough-as-shit pal, accomplished and worldly even, and mostly a best friend since pretty much forever—bent out of shape by her sister, an age-old comfortingly familiar story. Thank god.

She eagerly choked back a plug of snot. But, she said. What about Greg?

Greg who she liked to think of as Some-Greg, had been her friend's recent-at-the-time ex-ex. For a while, he'd also been her own. Suddenly she was not beyond imagining. Desire like melt, river runs throating deep-cut banks. A cock-salty, scorched-caramel scent to the stirring breeze. She was so there. And then she wasn't, her friend having paused long enough in the conversation for her to think the connection was a wash. Sleet pinged her windshield and she could hardly see. Her parents were still utterly recently dead. She considered yanking the car around at the first turn-off and heading back in the smoldering vile cold to the scene of the final break. She might never leave.

But her pal's voice suddenly resurfaced. You know Greg, she said. Greg is Greg.

Small world. Idiot world. Where was that turn-off? She transponded through a checkpoint, swung the wheel, gassed hard. Her car fishtailed then righted itself and she shot past all the fantabulous snow-wreathed digi-boards crowning the side of the road. Eat Here. Eat This.

God, her friend said after a moment's silence. I'm so sorry. Just listen to me.

Now, in the whack heat of late October, she nosed her car back along the cemetery's drive to the entrance. Still more listening to do. Still more amends to make, on her part and on her friend's too. But just before the main road she pulled over and got out. She washed her hands at the pump dedicated to some loved-one's memory and shook them dry. The sky had smogged over again. No sign of the white dots massing above. Once again her superpower, such as it was—to see the mostly unseen, to picture the body's inner dramas, her own version of watching and guarding—seemed blindingly flawed. Some power—what good had it done her parents in the end? Sometimes, when she momentarily forgot herself in her work, she'd suddenly snap back to this question. Worse, she'd imagine her parents asking the same question from beyond the grave, her mother a bewildered, sorrowful mist, her father a band pressed around her own chest or thighs. At least they were there, she thought as she shut her car's door and released the handbrake. At least they were still with her in whatever way they could be. Until this past week, when she'd bailed on them, or they on her.

You'd forget your own head, her mother used to tell her daughter. You'd forget if it wasn't screwed on so tight.

Turn signal on, she buzzed her window down. She could puke for guilt.

5

You're late, her friend Jane said.

She clutched her soda and slumped into a seat in the subterranean food court. Guilty as charged. She should have taken the subway after her meetings and debarked at her far station to board a private U!-shuttle. Having conducted her rituals, she could have swiftly returned, nursing a vitamin cocktail. Instead she'd grown increasingly woozy in her shushing sedan. The sky had darkened without warning and rain quick-silvered her windshield, transforming dips in the road to brimming goblets of mercury. Beautiful poison. She'd fought to keep her eyes open. Her ears rang. And now in Old Downtown—on the lowest concourse of a series of marble-columned malls that brambled beneath huge tracts of real estate—she felt sick. Just talking might kill her. Then again—she hazarded a glance and noted the swirling gold flecks in Jane's green irises—not talking might also kill.

Sorry, she finally said.

Jane jacked her elbows onto the table and rammed her fingers through her ice-pale hair. Her wide cheekbones and high forehead appeared glazed under the fluorescents. You and me both, she said. Dear Marilyn, you don't need to go there nearly every single day. I don't mean to be mean, but it's not like they're going anywhere.

Snick-snick—guilt and guilt. To cover, Marilyn sipped her drink. The over-lit concourse shrilled with laughter and reeked of rancid oil. Suit-clad men and women poured off the down escalator and flooded the concessions, though a few loose-limbed tee-shirted teenagers managed to crest through. So many so bright with hunger. She knuckled her eyes and wedged some soothing darkness in. She pinched her nostrils shut with her thumb and forefinger. A few claustrophobic seconds and she let go.

So? Jane said, launching an impatient, sculling motion with her hands. How come so out of touch?

Marilyn drank some more. Bottomless thirst. Just as, momentarily restored at her parents' graves today, she'd felt drained and lost once she'd turned onto the road. Very lost.

Don't think you're boring me, Jane continued— though already she seemed to be sighting the salad of shop signs in Franglish and Korean and Farsi that marked the bustling booths. Her narrow lips held the faint, aeons-familiar curl. Smile? Sneer? You're not boring me yet, she added, then offered a regal yawn.

A pang sat Marilyn upright. She liked to believe that if someone slit her open, inside might nest a near-semblance of her friend. Her Jane-twin. As kids on sleepovers at each other's houses, they'd fit like cut-outs, breathing each other's exhale. It seemed charged with the chlorophyll scent of frog-spawn that bolted in springtime from the banks of the forbidden creek— the waterway where on soggy fall days after school the terrible-twosome tormented muskrats into sewer pipes like the one in which Jane's older sister once paid them a dime to initiate them out of their knit tights and underpants so she could examine their girl parts. Years later there were the occasional boyfriends occasionally shared. The shared experience of bullshit jobs better than no jobs. Eventually better jobs and eventually even better-than-bullshit jobs.

Not lost. Not even this past grief-stricken year—not totally lost, thanks to Jane.

Okay, I'm doing him, Marilyn said. But it's not a big deal or anything.

And just saying it, it—he—wasn't. She suddenly felt cheated. Ashamed, as if she'd gorged on cotton candy. Double-ashamed. Not spun sugar—a person. She felt as if she'd disappeared him too.

Jane's face blanked. Who's him? she said, and bent and rummaged in the tote at her feet. Excellent, she went on in a muffled voice, not waiting for a reply. A diversion. That's what you want.

In Marilyn's mind, a familiar shredding eclipse so white it looked black. She glared at her friend. Who wants? she snarled.

Brandishing a giant pair of sunglasses, Jane shoved to her feet. She swooped in with a mock kiss then pushed the glasses onto the top of her head so that she appeared to possess two sets of eyes, the top ones reflecting the glances of passersby waiting to see what she might do next—if they'd been actual twins Jane would have been the bolder first-born. I love you, she said. But you're scaring me. I worry. Tell me you'll be fine.

The food-court din seemed to rise and recede and rebound off the marble pillars and granite-faced walls only to return in ever-louder circuits. Three, four stories underground? Marilyn only remembered the harried down and down. She quickly hooked her friend around her flexing waist. Jane had always turned every corner first, like some beautiful thrusting snake. But now Jane shifted out of Marilyn's grasp just as someone's shopping bag clunked her side. Hey, she groused after the someone, instead of responding to Jane's command. That kind of hurt.

Jane sighed. I'd love to stay, she said. But you have no idea the major stuff I have to do.

Marilyn winced. Earache, sick-of-self ache. With her usual patient impatience Jane co-directed a micro-agency that fed personnel to bureaus that serviced terror-ravaged consortiums desperately in need of insect netting to ward off dengue and malaria. Important work. Better than bullshit by a long shot. While Marilyn would only head home to ply her grisly trade reducing digital scans of diseased abdominal tracts to cross-sections, magnifying and shading ventricular septal defects, mining the inner lives of organs framed in tidy Exhibits A through Z like immaterial sarcophagi. Glyphs as substantial—since her parents' deaths—as scrapings of toast.

Jane pecked a hard one now on Marilyn's cheek and drew away. Marilyn experienced a sudden moment of double vision. In Jane's glasses, Marilyn's curves and hollows, her dark mat of difficult curls. Beneath the glasses, Jane cool and blonde, equally petite but trim-tight. The same and not-same, always. Marilyn an only child, Jane the middle of five, they'd grown up in houses kitty-corner to each other, another inverse proposition.

See you, Marilyn, Jane said, and vanished into the crowd.

Marilyn observed the condensation on her plastic cup. She fiddled with her obstinate hair, coarse as clustering weeds. Hurry. Run like a rat. Do something, don't fall behind. She stood, feeling like bottle fizz while the thousand artificial suns above her burned cold. An elderly, bird-beaked man appeared and pointed at her table. Taken? he said. Going or not?

Last night she had laid her head against her new interest's chest to hear its massive cargo beat. Why are you crying? she said, and brushed her fingertips over the blue pulsing along the side of his face and down his throat. She brought her fingers to her mouth for a second then continued to stroke his memorable skin—not only its blues but also where it was pitted and red in places as if brewed up from some hot spring and in others annealed in waxy moon-strips, souvenir of a somewhere she could hardly imagine. Or could—as with a jolt she suddenly craved the moment just before submerging. The moment just after.

She mumbled an apology to the waiting elderly man and blundered into the food court's criss-crossing hordes. She walked fast then faster. Her ears rang, her breath caught. She took shelter at a watch-repair stall. She caught her breath. Which way to the exit? She tried to glimpse her friend. Too late—no blond head flickering in the distance. She mouthed the ancient words anyway. See you, Jane.

6

The downstairs buzzer cut through the rain pounding on the roof above her third-floor apartment. He nestled the knife among the diced carrots and onions and wiped his hands on the dishtowel. Want me to get it? he said.

Expensive fish marinated on plates between his bottle of fancy beer and her second tumbler of white. Another shrill and he arched his barbed brows—well? Prize specimen. Oversized pinna and quashed nose. Asymmetrical trench carving a deep worry line into his forehead. On his barrel chest, sprays of grey and brown sprouting from the open vee of his white shirt. Sleeves rolled to display built arms. Medium height—possibly the only medium about him. Age—forty? Thirty? She hadn't asked yet and he hadn't offered. No blue tats tonight. They seemed to have a mind of their own.

You stay put, she said. Let's keep you stored right to the last possible.

He shrugged then swung back to the counter. Happy Halloween to you too, he said, hefting the knife again. Want me to hide in your closet while you and your friend chow?

She pressed against him from behind. I'm terrible, she said.

Yeah. What did I ever do to deserve?

But what had she done to deserve? The first night of his class—water to her navel, chilled in her swimsuit, only semi-paying attention to his bull-voiced harangue, something about the point and the how-to of the training exercise—she'd simply tried not to bang into the other neophytes. But the tank on her back dragged her off-balance and her fin-crippled feet hadn't helped. Last in line, waiting while one by one his students descended with him, she'd peered impatiently at the surface and discerned only smudges. No sign of the mysterious proficiencies he grudgingly acknowledged as each student resurfaced still in one piece. Finally he gargled her direction—next!— and she dropped. Her regulator chirred, breath exhaust burped. With her newfound tunnel vision, beefy boy-legs reverted to chubby infants' and princesses sported cruddy pimples along their groomed bikini-wax lines. Halogens glowed like portals along the pool's sides. And then two raps on her head. Pay. Attention. The point, the point. Something about something called mouth-piece retrieval. So she removed the apparatus from her mouth and tossed it. No air. She groped. Her suit-snuggy threatened to split her crack. A blur of hoses and fins, her own grasping fingers. What had ever tentacled around her and choked. Mr. Eliot in grade-eight math hypotene-using her low-grades ass into detention for a month. Her father's hand too tight around her fifteen-year-old's wrist for too long one afternoon in the dentist's waiting room. Mother's all-purpose refrain—no one will ever love you as much as your mother. All the memory-snow crazy. The inflated, wrong-headed. The concern too, the love—all the fucked-up riot love.

She'd suddenly stopped struggling. Chemicals stung her nasal cavities. Anguish runnelled her mind like rebar. For shame. How much she'd once ignored or fled. Allowed to evaporate. She felt ragged as a scarecrow cowering beneath a cement sky.

Until someone got hold of her bathing suit and hauled. Above—air, the menace of the world reinstating itself. She coughed, her snot streamed. Something scraped her right buttock. The divemaster—he had his head cocked in seemingly voracious surmise. Saliva build-up spooled along his cheeks and chin like a nearly transparent handlebar moustache. He opened his mouth and she could see down his shiny gullet. Still with me? he'd boomed.

High up in her third-floor apartment she clung to him from behind as he resumed chopping the vegetables. Maybe, she thought, her parents lay where she'd stored them, safe where she could find them. At the bottom of a pool. A small freshwater lake. A wherever apart from gravity's ordinary demands.

The apartment buzzer stabbed once more to life and she startled, wrist twisting painfully from the front of his pants. He quickly hoisted the kitchen knife high above the counter. Hey, he said, laughing. Careful, you.

She picked her way down the stairs and opened the front door. Elf, cowboy, pretty pony. Not-Janes. They cackled and shook tiny appendages. A rain-slickered woman wearing a pointy witch hat wielded a striped umbrella above her charges. Be nice, the woman warned.

Marilyn took up the candy bowl from the rickety entry-way table. So few kids trick-or-treated here that none of the other tenants of the converted-to-apartments ramshackle Edwardian even bothered to provide. But she had once been a pony and an escaped convict, and Jane a Jack-in-the-Box Jane who had grown up to now be officially late for dinner. If Jane showed at all, who might she be this time?

Beasts, I swear, the witch woman exclaimed at her charges. Enough! Be done!

The trio made off like bandits. Where they'd been stood a suddenly re-materialized best friend. She was sopping, clutching a soaked bunch of flowers while water ran off her nose, which she deigned to wipe.

Thanks for the invite, she said. Thought you'd never ask. Now if you'd be so kind, step aside and let me in.

Marilyn made no move. Please, she said. Can't you just for once be nice?

Ha. Some trick.

Jane, I'm only begging.

Jane ramrodded her free arm in front of her, aiming right at Marilyn's chest. Coming through, Madam, she said. Coming through.

Inside the foyer Jane dripped on the worn parquet and sniffed the air. She thrust the bouquet of orange mums forward then licked her pale lips. So can I change? she said. I appear to have come as a puddle.

Jane, Rand. Rand, Jane.

Done and done, Jane said to Marilyn. Happy now?

Rand poured Jane some wine and held the glass out to her. Not so bad, is it? he said.

Not so, Jane allowed.

He held his beer up for a toast. Here's to not so, he said.

7

Dessert. Thunder boomed outside and echoed in the cavernous living-dining room and the windows clattered in their loose frames. The bulbs in the chipped chandelier blinked off and on—the district's next scheduled brownout wasn't until the following evening but whole cheap-rent blocks like hers sometimes darkened with no warning and she'd switch to her stores of battery reserves and race to meet her deadlines before her back-up power drained. Rand—who was now waving his fork across the table at Jane—happened to live in one of the more affluent enclaves, whose grids he happened to underground for his day job. He was an electrical engineer with a lot of quality training and a fine income with excellent benefits including a flexible work schedule with decent time off, so Marilyn had taken to feeling no compunction in blaming him for her own inadequate power situation. Plus, now he'd allowed Jane to irk him throughout the meal.

So why not your social-action tourism right here at home? he demanded of Jane in some kind of counter-attack.

Good luck with that. As if Marilyn even knew about this other-Jane—a younger one, just out of college and kicking it in an ocean-side drought-land of gated oases and armed insurrections and kidnappings, of resistant strains this and influenza that. Her devout-yet-non-missionary family had nearly died just contemplating. She was gone a year give or take, a time about which she rarely spoke, and the longest gap in their friend-ship. Marilyn's fault. Overwork learning to visualize the bio-pathogenic status updates of the body brought to her fresh weekly from autopsies at med-school complexes. And also the overwork in those days—she admitted it now—of her own version of crummy self-absorption. A bad boyfriend or three. Bad parenting, she'd been sure at the time, from her squalling, over-involved mother and father. You never write, you never call, they called frequently to complain. True, she hadn't called them much, and increasingly at the time not Jane either. Marilyn had let her hair grow greasy, missed classes, barely graduated a semester late. She deserved Jane's heel now digging into her thigh—Jane almost lying in her chair on the same side of the table as her friend, one leg atop hers as if she were an ottoman.

So what did you do out there anyway? Rand went on when Jane ignored his question.

Marilyn squirmed as much as Jane allowed her. Rand, let up, Marilyn said, though secretly she herself wanted to know the answer too.

Nothing much, Jane said, addressing Marilyn. Scrubbed rich dicks' toilets. Organized a health collective.

Marilyn's ears burned and buzzed. Her thigh throbbed and she massaged Jane's instep in hopes of preventing further bodily harm while Rand scoured the tines of his fork over his plate. That noise. Marilyn resisted the urge to screech at him.

So you did something, he said. Or tried to. Good for you.

Jane removed her leg from Marilyn's and shifted toward him. So what about you? she said. Lord of the Underworld and all that. All for personal thrills and chills?

Marilyn yanked at the cake plate and dolloped some frosting onto her finger, which she then wagged. Another slice, kiddos? she said warningly. Jane, small?

Unlikely, Jane said, though she did appear no bigger than a girl in Marilyn's borrowed tee and jeans.

By the way, I see how this is going, he said, smirking.

How is this going? Jane said.

Marilyn swept the hair from her neck and shook it. Kind of hot in here, she said.

Do not, Jane said, still facing him down. Leave me alone with him. Ever. Unless you're going for more booze.

The candle flames from the votives lining the table guttered low. Jane's mums emitted coppery cones of light. The rain had let up and the room seemed even more echoey and vast. Blame her recent ear infection, Marilyn thought, which seemed to clear only after a course of potent off-label antibiotics she'd purchased at a storefront down the street.

Crunch diving, Jane was saying, and her voice seemed to come from a long way off. I like the lingo. So what's it like in the really small caves?

His big head appeared to bobble slightly on his neck. Like diving for hours inside a coffin, he allowed.

Jane set aside the tangerine peel she'd been playing with and snorted. If it's so bad, why do it? she said.

To know you can. To push your limits. Feel more alive.

Jane gazed at the ceiling, lightly tapped her fingers on the table. What about her? she finally said. For starters, tell me she's not going to solo dive like you.

Okay, he said. Here's how it works. Contrary to what you might have heard, the buddy system's just an excuse for being poorly trained. Think somebody else will be there to bail you out? That's just wishful thinking that the other person will be more competent than you. And that's no better than leaving things to chance. To luck. Which should have nothing to do with it. Even Marilyn here, with just a baby course and one dive under her belt, should tell the buddy system to piss off.

Huh, Jane said. Quite the speech, guy.

He pushed back from the table, folded his arms over his chest, smiled.

Baby? Marilyn swallowed more drink. She'd forgotten what a blowhard he could be in class. But this was next-level bullshit.

Anyway, isn't not having a buddy against rules? Jane said.

There's a higher set of rules.

Who makes those? Who gets to decide?

Those who do. The ones who have the know-how. Not the ones who like to police what they know nothing about.

I've heard this kind of thing before, Jane said.

Marilyn poured herself another big one. She felt blurry and fierce and fucked with. Fuck him. So why are you teaching the babies? she said, enunciating with care. Like me. Why lower yourself?

He unfolded one of his shirtsleeves and buttoned the cuff. What I just said, he said after a pause. People at all levels should be better trained. Self-sufficient. Besides, I'm not advocating technical diving for everyone.

She took another slug and wiped her mouth with the back of her hand. You mean, for me, she said. Really? Because?

Really, he said. Because the stakes are pretty fucking high.

She polished off her drink. Not that she harboured any real ambitions for the kind of diving he was talking about—not that she held any idea about it at all. But why limit herself? Why should he limit her? What stakes? she said.

He worked on his other shirtsleeve even more slowly than the first as if to suggest a tensile economy earned at some expense, the need to make his showboat words sound like an understatement. Only when he was done did he flip her a brief, unreadable look. For a second, blue teased at his temples. I've lost people, he said. Friends. That answer your question?

She'd lost people too, she knew all about that. Okay, she said sharply. I guess I hear you.

Don't get me wrong, he said, holding his hands palm up then dropping them. You're doing good. You don't panic. You wait and think through the situation. That's a skill to bank on. It's what first impressed me about you.

She picked the bottle off the table. Empty. She put it back and downed her water instead. Maybe she was what he saw. Or maybe she could become that.

To Marilyn doing more good, Jane said and raised her glass. Rand joined her. Marilyn did too, though she had nothing left to swallow.

8

The rain had let up and the slick streets thrummed with lights from cars and jumbled storefronts. Goblins and celebrity hosts and former dictators jostled by in the river air porous with the smells of garbage and fried food and grilled meats. A driver blammed on the horn and fists shook. A squad of taxis loosened and eased away. She launched into the breach after one. A bike flotilla loomed. Bells and curses rang. Easy, Jane said and with a squeeze to the scruff of the neck righted Marilyn onto the sidewalk.

She shook herself off. I am only trying to get you home, she said very slowly. Since you refused his ride.

Marilyn, I stayed because I, unlike a certain someone, wanted to make sure you were okay. Okay? And you don't have to shout.

I'm not shouting. But if you want me to I will.

They stepped aside to let a dishevelled man pushing a cart of rags pass. Fast-moving figures like wasp-filled jars buzzy with energy approached and vanished behind. Some enchanted evening. The drink, but maybe also labyrinthitis. Or cerebellar tumors like the diagrammed nodules she needed to spiff pronto in the next week for a particularly picky textbook-consortium client—just thinking about the job wearied her to the point of exhaustion so she let Jane grip her hand and tow her through the wait-line at the taqueria counter, past the carts selling pirated handsets and off-off medications, the vegan automat. Near the pocket-library Marilyn managed to loop her arm through Jane's and halted, halting Jane. The sidewalk continued, though— it appeared to eddy out from under them while Jane appeared to feign ignorance. Above and beyond the nearby bridge the freeway splashed more traffic and, higher still, dragonfly helicopters slalomed among the condo sky-plinths. Barges slid below on the oily river. Anyway, Jane said, with her free hand scooping Marilyn's curls off her clammy forehead. It's you and me now.

He was being polite, Marilyn said. Giving us our space. Or do you not even know what polite is?

Smatterings of applause like firecrackers broke out and a group of buskers began to crackle notes that sounded like glaze cracking on a cup. Marilyn, Jane said with a laugh. Are we having a fucking fight?

No we're not. Wait, I'm sorry. Yes. Yes we are. Fuck yes.

Jane's arm slackened in Marilyn's. A falsetto of sirens sang out on a nearby street and she recalled another busy sidewalk, five years ago, just before Jane high-tailed it out of town for thirteen months, lank with misery. Some trouble—pregnant? Hard to hear. Too much noise. Marilyn had coughed and excused herself. You bitch, Jane said after her as Marilyn scurried off. Call me. But Marilyn had work and more work and her Amir-trouble too—Amir the poet-painter, sweetheart of several seemingly serene co-habitation months before he transplanted to the West Coast with a clean-break vengeance of which she hadn't thought him capable. And before Amir she'd had her Stephen-months. But she'd always had Jane. Right? Jane pregnant? Not possible. And then not possible but somehow cowardly true Marilyn's not calling. Jane's counter-silence lasted a month—crazy, impossible—which stretched to seven weeks then the time away that Rand had just questioned her about. Call me, you bitch. But in the end it was Jane who'd called.

The street sirens neared and a security pod whipped past on their PTs. Jane gently unhooked her arm from Marilyn's. Unsupported, she swayed on her feet. What if Jane had never called? Marilyn's mind suddenly foamed. Panic flooded her throat.

Wait, she said again. I'm sorry. Really sorry.

Liar, Jane said with some tenderness, and added a conciliatory hip-check. You're a menace, Marilyn.

A menace all right. Each day during Jane's absence had increased Marilyn's paralysis. Six months after their meet-up on the sidewalk it was Jane's older sister, running into Marilyn in a coffee shop, who'd finally alerted her. Jane in the Pacificas while Marilyn mostly squirrelled away in her hidey hole, in thrall to a mercifully dispassionate precision regarding the articular capsule and sacral nerve. Until Jane initiated the truce. Back from her adventure, her good works, but the same-Jane in that—with the exception of their soon-to-be shared unremarkable Greg—her guys bore names and faces Marilyn rarely troubled herself with except maybe over popcorn before the start of a movie. How's Colin? What's up with your Magana? And Jane would only clam.

Now Marilyn's head reeled. She needed to lie down. I'm a fuck-up, she said. I know it. But can we please just keep going?

Two laughing girls sheared by and a filthy child darted after them, shaking a cup. The buskers resumed busking and Marilyn imagined each musician beneath their clothes, tambourining their bone suits. With a sudden massing of helicopters above the river, light strewed on the festive filthy current and crumbling aqueduct. Marilyn pictured herself and Jane as old women hunched like aged crows on the river's far bank, eyes hooded and watching—ruthlessly watching—their younger selves preen past.

Sure, Jane said. But you better crash at my place.

Jane and Jane and Jane, Marilyn thought. She'd let her parents go as if they were strangers, unaccompanied and uncomforted to their deaths. Her mother in intensive care, alone except for medicals in the middle of the night. Marilyn's father frantic with grief and beelining unattended to the nearest crowd for cold solace on a rush-hour subway ride he otherwise had no need of taking. And Jane—Marilyn had abandoned her once too.

Marilyn slunk forward, hoping her friend might follow for a change. Right, she said, mimicking an airy tone. She hoped! She said, Let's just not talk about what I never did.

PART TWO

9

Jane knelt on the rollicking deck and pulled an item from her toolbox. She reached out her hand. A small silicone ring studded her palm. Here, she said. Allow me.

Bile clawed Marilyn's throat. A tangle of grey messed the horizon and screaming gulls lurched in the wind. Save it, she said.

Jane's torso seemed to flick back and forth as the boat bucked. She stretched her arm farther in Marilyn's direction and shook it. Just take it, Jane said.

Only a few excursions left—maybe only today's—before the late season slammed shut the whole enterprise until next summer. But Marilyn's planned big dive now looked like major asshat. What couldn't go wrong? Motion sick. A blown O-ring in one of her tank valves and lucky her she'd failed to restock her kit. A loud round with her husband over her apparent unprepared bullshit before he skulked into the cabin where the crew and other divers congregated out of the bluster in a space so tight it seemed teeth might knock. Leaving Jane to the rescue. Although something of a novice still, she was fully suited already, her black hood pinching her face and whitening her lips. Unlike Marilyn's, Jane's rig was ready and lashed to the boat's hull with bungee cords. Jane closed her fingers now on the proffered ring. You're right, she said. Call it. You're stressed. Or dive with me instead. Very chill, like yesterday. I promise.

Nausea swelled Marilyn's gut like something grappling to get out. Two intense years of diving told her she just needed to get down fast, beneath the surface commotion, beneath the waves. So she opened her mouth to the scouring wind, stalked forward and dug the ring from her friend's fist.

That was yesterday, Marilyn said.

Hey, Jane said, shaking her fingers. I'm not the enemy. Remember?

First one in, Marilyn hung. Alien, aquanaut—trussed and bound, packed tip to toe into a sealed drysuit. Hoses from her tanks tentacled around her and a nylon harness cradled her chest and hips and crotch and cupped her buoyancy device to her back like wings. Above, wave-stitched seams. Below, mud. Rising from that mud, the wreck, a chance to commune with a hulking carcass of wood and steel. But here, twenty feet beneath the surface in a pewter-tinted corona of visibility that extended maybe thirty feet in all directions before blurring like smoke—thirty-foot viz—just water, water, everywhere. Freshwater. Middle of the north channel between two great northern lakes. Marilyn tightened her grip on the derricking down-line. It tethered the floating buoy—to which the converted fishing tug was tied—to a concrete plug sunk in the muck next to the busted freighter. She took it on faith that the boat with the other divers and crew remained where she left it, that the wreck she'd dived as recently as yesterday with Jane remained. Marilyn closed her eyes, worked out a hitch in her breathing. God forbid she ever keep Rand waiting. She opened her eyes again. The underside of waves a shimmering twill.

He came at her from above, a hooded figure descending in a brocade of bubbles. But when he arrived it was fast and hard with a bang to her shoulder, growling through his regulator. Then he was gone. Monkeyfuck. She caught herself and carefully tilted. His ascending breath reached her like the detached bones of a beckoning hand. A bell chimed in her head. Going down?

She fell. Immense pressure. Her suit squeezed like a pelt. She swallowed compulsively as if hiccupping and her ears popped as she struck through strata of increasingly frigid temps like walls of frost. Not falling—winging through the thermoclines and thickening blackness while the down-line slid in measured increments through her glove. At seventy feet the dark mushroomed. She slowed and unhooked the head of her powerful main light from her harness and with a twist of the handle the beam swept on. Below and beyond, faintly illumined cumulous wisped through inky fields.

Ninety-seven feet according to her wrist-mounted, LED-lit computer. End of the line. Fog—her brain on the nitrogen from her increasingly pressurized air. She peered through the haze and soon spied the second rope. It slanted off the main line into mist. She followed the new rope's slow rise and soon the outline of a railing materialized—and Rand. Glowering? His dim shape seemed to resolve with that of the ship, as if both were composed of the bottom's endless silt. She swam toward him. At the railing she hovered, rechecked her pressure gage and computer. She recalled the location of her back-up regulator and secondary computer, the duplicate mask, bezel watch and laminated decompression tables stored in a zippered pouch on her waistband, mentally summoned the ship's schematics, which she'd studied this past summer. She was here—upper level of the port-side bow. As if flipping a switch, the sequence of cognitive tasks snapped her synapses back on. She flooded alert. The cove of brightness extended as far as the lights she and Rand shone. She made eye contact with him and he nodded and in a freeing aphasia they began their flyover.

They glided over the ship's broad deck. The colossal windless, the anchor chains like giant steel-forged braids disappearing into the hawse pipes. The starboard railing. Further aft, toward the downward-sloping stern where the lakebed plunged deeper, the open windows of the forecabins. Here she slowed and swung her beacon. He pulled alongside. What? She spotlit her palm, vertical now and facing out. Wait. She pointed a finger to her mask. Watch. Humour me, hard-ass. She dropped over the hull and descended ten, fifteen feet and then scanned upward. No luck. No money shot—a view of the massif silhouetted by faint ambient light filtering from the surface. But no harm trying. So what if she'd have to deal with him post-dive. Like she'd never done that before. She stroked the vessel's skin. Well over a century's worth of grime membraned away and she considered the sobering development, the bitter arc—steaming along and then not. Likely scuttled—newspaper accounts of the day reported that before departing, the underfed crew hawked most of the detachables, the sinking snuffed no lives, and the First Great Depression was on, with insurance claims far more valuable than a cargo of creaky leather boots and one-inch nails few could afford. And so this commercial freighter—built in 1888 by the Globe Iron Works—ended abandoned, wrecked.

Something pulled in Marilyn like a weight. She exhaled and sank, feeling soft as pillows on a cold dark night—a sleepless night, the alone hours she sometimes missed since the shack-up, time that used to stretch to reveal her mother's raucous nicotined laugh, father straightening the knot in a new tie and mock-demanding, Who's your handsome papa? Now Marilyn inhaled deeply, filling her lungs, and rose along the hull toward Rand and their planned dive. Within feet though something caught her eye. Another eye, blinking. She stopped. A mud puppy maybe nine inches long—aquatic salamander uncommon though not unheard of in such cold. Little wonder, really. A wreck rebirthed as host—in no way uncommon. She drew closer to the creature. Pudgy tail barely distinguishable from attenuated legs. Sledgehammer head. Mushroomy ruff of gills. Except for that first telltale movement, the antediluvian nervous system seemed paralyzed in her light's glare.

Another blink. *Enchanté.*

In this bijou moment—hers, all hers—the sizzle of singularity.

A blurred shout jolted her. A forceful thump dislodged her mask and icy water gushed in. Breath throttling in her reg, she wedged her shoulder against the hull to steady herself and clear her faceplate. A basic skill to cancel the insult—hardly an injury—of forcing her attention as one might a fear-impaled novice under pressure of being under pressure. Thanks, jerk. Silt swarmed her like flies at a feast. Zero viz. Wait it out, she told herself. Let the crap settle. Give the bastard a scare.

Or call it, as Jane had suggested—not just this dive but diving with him period. She'd soloed flooded quarries and mines and magnificent submerged limestone caves, and one cave formed entirely of rough-edged marble. She'd tootled stag through salty warm seas stocked with bejeweled corals and blue tang and damselfish, companionless braved the bilious North Atlantic until clouds of transparent, broken-backed shrimp crowned aureoles around her drowsy, decompressing head that felt liquid as the element in which she was immersed. Solo was a desirable option. Or partner with others more like herself, or more novice. Jane, for example.

But alone or re-partnered meant slow and steady training, baby steps which rankled the pride she'd only recently, these past two years, discovered she possessed—while love's tight, scratchy fit took her farther faster. Each holy-shit-complicated excursion with Rand led to a re-stitched seam of the surface, a thing as freshly remade as her newly accomplished self. The two of them together another surprise—never so close, his post-dive bulk seeming to swell in her arms. Both of them sweeping aside the tedious task of figuring who'd done what to who, and why. Together replacing the unvoiced *why go on at all with each other?* with *why stop now?*

Enough. She rose above the waning silt-cloud to the deck's railing, to the wheelhouse slumped to one side like a rotting haystack in a long-fallowed field. To Rand. He regarded her then shrugged. In response she thrust two fingers forward. Let's go. Soon the other, lesser-skilled divers from the boat would spasm by and the viz would drop. Jane would be down.

She finned toward the ship's deeper-lying stern. It soon cliffed into view—as did, beyond and slanting ever deeper, the lakebed's non-navigable underwater dunes, marker-less and disorienting. And so, tailed by Rand she hugged the hull as she crossed over the vessel's half-buried massive propeller. Portside she located the entrance with her beam, and nudged in. The greater darkness swallowed some of her wattage. She focused on an interior doorway immediately to her left, knowing from previous dives that this led to a corridor lined with the tiny quarters for the crew. The brief concentrating cleared her head. And then with a few careful frog kicks, mindful of the accumulated silt, she soon arrived at the descending staircase to the engine room—where the real dive would begin.

10

She hung back while he unclipped a four-inch reel from his harness. He unspooled some of the thin nylon and wrapped it several times around the top of the steel banister and tied off. Then he reefed down the narrow stairs, running the line behind. Within seconds a rust blizzard stormed up. She clutched the railing with one hand to keep her bearings. When the sleeting orange flakes engulfed her, she began to grind down too—sightless, head first, on hands and knees. Catch, release, pick, unpick. Metal scraped metal. No surviving a torn hose or whacked-open tank valve—her air fluming at once into the slosh would mean game over in less than a minute. And yet there was no turning back on this freeze-frame rollercoaster—too tight here to have second thoughts and scooch around. She ticked down each step like a cog in the gear-work of fright, claustrophobia nipping her brain, but she soon beat it back by calming her breathing, felt herself expand to fit the contours her body normally made. In the zero viz her optic nerves still fired, shaping the sprawling silt and rust into jagged, grasping edges. A crying mouth like a cyst. Mother crooning rock-a-bye. Father's throat-bob swallow before opening a present—a comb she bestowed when she was six. Gone but still here until she shut her eyes against them.

She opened her eyes again—only a gummy mess.

Soon the tightness yielded and she stubbed her elbows on what must be floor. She pushed off with her arms, lofting several inches, and stroked once with her fins. Just past the slag lay a kettle-black midnight scummed with white foam. Narcosis. She needed to find his line, and right now. The engine room likely seethed in tortuous switchbacks among bashed, silt-coated machines. Snagged on some instrument or machine, unable to free herself in the murk, she'd hoover her air to zip. Or freed, blindly search for the exit while sucking her tanks dry. Drown or drown. Great fat chances. She peered through the narcosis and screen of whitish particulate with a rabid ferocity as if to will the line into being. She'd done it before. In other tough situations underwater—head addled by the cold, the dark, the depth—by the sheer force of mental power, she'd conquered, survived by finding what she needed. Just as she sometimes willed her parents still alive into her dreams.

The line, the line.

There. She edged toward the filament. Here. Now she immediately studied her pressure gage and computer. One hundred twenty-two feet. Twenty-three minutes since she first hit the water. Instantly her revived mental processes burned off the narcosis brume. In its place appeared heaped silt-mandalas in greys and bitter browns. Steel beams blistered like delicate arabesque carvings. Half a foot from the ceiling, Rand. Watching her, suspended like a giant spider from a thread. A second of eye contact then he signalled. Okay? Okay. He turned and swam, continuing to run the reel. She eased behind him through the labyrinth. Their breath-exhaust burped upward, dislodging ferrous debris the size of poker chips, a darting lingcod with its spiky barbel beard. Finally, at the ship's immense boilers she placed her cold-numbed hand against the lip of the furnace, once stoked with a robber-baron's wealth of blazing coal, and he closed a glove over hers. They hung together, locked in a high-wire stillness, inside an inside revealed to an unrivalled few.

Finally she jiggled her hand and he released her. They both rechecked their gages. Soon they'd reach the safe limits of their breathing mix and planned downtime. She circled now with her forefinger pointing up. Dive over. A yes from him and she again followed the line, threading among the lurching objects while he reeled in behind. A few minutes and they returned to the silt-hole obscuring the bottom of the stairs. Hard to believe that through this brackish soup, impenetrable by her powerful primary light, lay the exit. And yet better believe, she told herself, bracing for the inevitable—the way in was the way out. No other choice. So once again she backed and forthed and upped and downed, bumbling on her hands and knees, every breath a vicious belch. The space seemed to increasingly narrow, as if she were funnelling in a reverse-tornado. A trick too this sense of timelessness—that she'd always been here, exerting herself, that all else had been but façade, mystery.

Then she reached the top of the stairs. She clutched the railing again and swung backward, into sight.

She waited at the top of the stairs. Soon he would re-emerge and unwrap the line. They'd swim out together. All the way out, to open water. Eventually air—and ballooning above, the indigos and magentas and every shade in-between of the terrestrial world. On the dive boat's deck, alternating swigs of energy drinks and beer and crude dumb jokes, a muzzy camaraderie among the dearly returned. Good one, Jane? Yeah, you too? And a moment when Marilyn would take her husband by the chin and observe the waxy polish of his eyes—symptom of the residual narcosis still lacing the bloodstream—and suppose it mirrored hers. She'd trace her hand over his unmasked face and explore the plains and gullies of his extraordinary features, feel the cold rise like marsh gas off his stubble, note the briefest blue shapes pulsing in his temples—indulge herself with such confections. Queen to his king. No one else on board would have pulled off the same dive. She'd lay her head against his considerable chest and inhale the tart scent of his suit. Fanning the grandiosity, she'd bask on deck, rain or shine, the cruise home like a triumphal procession. She knew, she knew. But didn't she deserve? Over everything, a narcotic sheen like a silvery web. A pleasant spell lingering in the tissues and cortical pathways, the wrinkles and arcane pleats of the brain.

Waiting, she relaxed. The real dive was done.

11

Hypothermia struck fast. The longer she waited the more she chattered at her mouthpiece. She knew the danger. Feeling increasingly colder she'd breathe harder and, with the increased nitrogen in her bloodstream, her mind would go dark and darker. To wake her sluggish blood she swam into the nearby corridor and finned past a few cubby-sized rooms. She thrust her light inside one. Ochre-stained sink. A cupboard door off its hinge. Four tiny bunks. Rust tinted the water the sepia of old photographs sold cheap at flea markets—abandoned images of bun-haired progenitors, bushy-bearded patriarchs, genetic pre-histories in nose shapes and cheekbones, stooped shoulders, adversity-resistant gazes. Shivers racked her again. If only she could stay awhile despite the cold. If only she didn't need to keep moving, owned unlimited gas, limitless downtime. If her husband wasn't going to show any second and bust her again—for what, again?

*

In the floating place.

Childhood dog swimming alongside her in a lake, wet snout upthrust, snorting like a water dragon—please let me never forget, she remembered begging herself at the time. Another time, sick with having swallowed an ant, realizing too late as she pigged the cookie wickedly proffered by Jane's older sister. Never again. Time too that Marilyn, bedevilled by hot greed, gobbled Jane's doughnut on the school bus—Jane's attention momentarily drawn to something out the window—and shame-sick recognized the lesson learned. Time of mumps-sick and feverish in bed, the slow lightning of the wallpaper's repeating ivory roses, hiving vanilla cupcakes, Ferris wheels—brought to mind years later by Jane's drifting hair a slow-spinning craquelure on the surface of the pool and then dissolving as she disappeared under for the first time, first dive class under Rand's tutelage and Marilyn's proud assist. Disappeared too the lush childhood ravine cut with creek water, that creek eventually bulldozed under, long gone. A snowflake's brief sharp prism at mother's funeral turned to dog dander, dog grown gimcrack, beloved muzzle massaged as the vet put him down. Or father's drained exasperation each time he called his daughter a chub during her pre-teen years. Mother's favourite ashtray whipped at Marilyn's late-teen head the night cops drove her home, having found her high and bumping into parked cars on her return from a high-school party. The pilling on Dad's most festive wool socks, worn every winter Saturday. In spring, mother in the yard with a baseball bat, laughing at her daughter's wild pitch, the ball at rest among a rapture of daffodils.

*

Stay. No one will ever love you as much. A lullaby never-again like a lantern she brandished farther inside the wreck. One more small berth and then one more and she'd turn back—not much time left here, she knew, she wasn't stupid. But in the precious minutes allotted her she'd take what she could get. Hers, all hers, all of it, the bad with the good. All aboard.

As if possessed she angled her light beam, gridding and slicing with surgical precision into each compartment, parting and parsing nothing and nothing. Something— an abandoned rubber boot overflowing with a fountain of mud. Stunning sight. Something to kill for. To die.

She took the hit like a dial-twist to static—atomized flight into silt, then full-stop in a grey fizz. No up, no down. She vibrated blindness. Took a moment to realize how hard she sucked her reg. So she knew—still breathing, still here.

Here but she wanted out. This instant. The urge struck to strip free from her gear. As if that was what trapped her here. Another instant and she regained some of her reason. The way in, the way out. Think, she thought from some pit deep in her brain. Think hard or die. Had any thought ever been clearer? Think and live.

For a second she relapsed, panted with want. Mom, Dad. But they were gone to pieces with nothing to put them together again.

Breath gurgling like something wounded, she fought her way back to that stone centre in her skull, its pure-cold imperatives. She willed herself to slow her breathing so that more thoughts could enter her head. They rooted there, enlarged her, pushing against the prison of her panic as her sense of possibilities grew. Will what you want to see, she told herself. Live! And so she groped at the hoses fastened to her chest, vented her wings— and with a bang discovered floor. And so knew up from down. A start. She stretched an arm. Nothing, and with it the sense she might thin herself like an ever-diminishing, unrecalled ghost. She smothered the thought. She located her belly—her body, still here—and crawled forward not knowing where forward might be, but searching at least, making a new starting point. So she inched along. Nothing and more nothing. Then wall. More wall. She nearly wept with wall. And when it disappeared she nearly cried in rage. Room? Stumble into one and increase the already frenzied silt and get more lost, breathe her tanks dry. And just thinking she choked again with fear, her mind a derangement of shrinking origami.

And so thinking she refused to think more. Just count, she urged herself. Breathe in three seconds. Three out. Here were her gut and arms and legs. She spanned both arms. Wall and then wall. Her chest vast as air. All she needed.

Then another topple through space, until a sliver of emerald stayed her.

12

Light. The above-world filtering dimly down through a crack in the wreck. She wallowed toward it. Only when she closed in did it register that the chink angled sharply, maybe a whole foot. Not much but she'd take it. Undo her harness, shed her gear. Reg gripped between her teeth, push her rig through and then squeeze herself after. Finally out, don her rig again for the swim back to the rope and make her ascent. She'd survive.

A strange transformation overtook her. Every part of her contracted. She became a dark lens with the slit of light as her iris.

She reached it. She felt irradiated by warmth. And then—as if her mind had suddenly fused and she'd rotated into another, gleaming dimension—the cleft yawned. Not a cleft. The narrowest side of a fully propped-open hatchway. Dear lord. So frozen with fear her peripheral vision had narrowed to a shred, she'd nearly missed her escape. She swam for it now.

She lay on the aft deck as if gutted, feeling loosened inside, depleted as if she'd just given birth to herself. Bubbles poured off the hull from hairline fractures—her recently spent breath still seeking an exit, as if another her were left behind. But some of the bubbles gained force and shifted. They travelled in a straight line along the corridor toward the bow. Faint light flickered the same course. Jesus god. She rose to her knees. Silt catacombed up from the door below the deck. She crawled again and when she reached the side of the wreck dropped back down. In between the cascading waves of muck she found Rand's line now tied to the outside railing and threading inside. Where he swam, seeking her out and using his line in a basic safety protocol—don't get lost in attempting a rescue, don't end with two deaths instead of one. The realization fanged in her—she should have run her own line before entering the corridor, and not gotten lost to begin with. At the very least, once lost she should have used her reel—attached by a clip to one of the stainless rings on her harness—to tie to something inside before searching for the exit. That way she wouldn't have risked getting more lost. With an effort now she tacked her mind back to the main fact of the moment—her husband. Still inside, still probing the darkness for her.

She forced herself to make touch-contact with the filament. She needed to re-enter, locate and retrieve him. But debris continued to billow around her and, fighting the irrational urge to hold her breath, she froze. And then the line between her nearly frigid thumb and index finger suddenly jerked violently and she let go and crabbed back.

He exited, silt steaming from him. They ogled each other as if they'd each stuck their heads in a massive socket. She lost all sense of where she ended and he began.

The feeling quickly passed. His features contorted behind his mask and his bulk seemed to gain mass. She stuck out a paw and, heaving into her reg, launched off the hull and soon passed the wheelhouse, the mainmast. She barely startled when he overtook her near the fore-cabins, no comment. Gone.

She reached the rope. Like an oversized umbilicus, it led to the surface—to the buoy, the boat. She extinguished her main light. Instead of ascending she lurked in the semi-dark, oddly here, she thought, as if she were still trapped. As if part of her were still deep down, inside the wreck. What if she stayed down? What if the part of her that was here re-entered the wreck? She could join her other half, nestle into some forgotten closet and curl in for the count. Suckle her tanks dry while drowsing thanks to late-stage hypothermia's illusion of warmth. Worse ways to go, she thought, shaking so hard now from the cold she thought her bones might break. She listened to the wreck creak—it seemed as if it were chir-ruping toward her. Nothing else was, at least. Probably the other divers had long ago made their way to the boat. Rand wouldn't be there yet though, not with his long decompression deficit, a lengthy one like hers. But if she waited here long enough, adding to her deco, with any luck she'd miss him.

She checked and rechecked her gas supply and then, little option left, finally began her ascent. No rapture, no glory. Just ninety and then seventy and sixty feet. At fifty she reached her first decompression stop according to the display on her computer. She held onto the rope, hovering face first and parallel to the now-invisible bottom, while she off-gassed some of the surfeit of nitrogen in her bloodstream. No getting bent. At least there was that. A few dazed minutes and she continued to her next stops, resting in ten-foot increments for increasingly longer periods. At twenty she swapped her air for the O2 reg the crew had run out from the boat and clipped to the line to aid in swabbing the unwanted gas from her circulation. She performed her air breaks at fifteen-minute intervals, changing from one reg back to the other. Her computer cleared her for ten feet. Last stop, more than an hour's worth. Hang time. She jiggered unthinkingly in the eerily glowing water, vacantly observed sunlight spindle down. So the weather had improved though rumbles and slaps echoed from the tug as steel battered waves. She needed to pee, badly. She switched gases like clockwork. Finally her computer cleared her. Open wide, she thought as she broke the surface and entered the burning sky.

13

She entered another maze.

She'd fucked up. She was fucked up. In his view, which he didn't hesitate to elaborate, cutting her off mid-stammer, shouting over the diesel roar. Port side? Try starboard, dear. And try this. She'd trashed the viz when he finally found her in back of the corridor. When he tried to stir her stupefied butt back to life and surprise, surprise all hell broke loose. Imagine his surprise—all that trouble to hustle her down there and keep her from ape-shitting all over the place. Remember the plan? Which she'd fucked with from the start. Did she not remember that as well? Sinking to the bottom off the bow and staring at the mud like a total whack-job. He was not fucking joking.

She was not fucking laughing. She planted her legs widely beneath her, beside her rig lashed to the hull with bungee cords—which she could hardly see in the explosion of sun off the white deck of the ram-jamming boat. Her sinuses streamed. The fuck? He was confused. She knew where she'd been.

The tug trenched and soared and his craggy face swung near then farther from her. Behind him she glimpsed Jane, blond hair like a sparkler in the ravenous light—in high relief to the cabin's extinguishing shade where the other divers and the crew had slunk the second Marilyn scrabbled aboard.

At this point, I think you don't know squat, he declared. What are you, a tourist? Where was your safety line? If you can't do a dive like this, dear, you should hang up your fins. Stay home and bake cookies.

You'd like that?

He mashed his palms together and arrowed his fingertips at her. You, he said. Fucking. Do not. Get it.

She tried to dodge him and her calves smashed against a storage box—hers, she saw when she hazarded a glance. He un-tented his hands and jabbed a finger inches from her nose.

One, he said. You didn't know where you were.

I did know, but so what? That's not the point here.

He held up two fingers. You didn't follow the plan, he said.

Forget the plan, she protested. Unless you planned what really happened. What you did.

His face reddened in patches around his pale scars. I'll tell you what never really happened, he raged, sticking three fingers at her. You never ran a line. Never used your fucking safety reel.

It seemed as if the tug's movement suddenly ceased. A white wing hung motionless in mid-flight against the sky. Smell of diesel and creosote. Out on the expanse of water, small islands like wells of rock in a vast liquid field. Silence on board, though she knew the tug's engine was near-deafening. Jane's dazzle near the cabin door. Then a cloud sailed in front of the sun and somehow restarted the keel-pounding boat-toss. He waved both arms now as if dismissing her. She stood her ground though his jaw and neck bulged and his lips curled as if he were chomping hot stones. Get your head back on, he shouted. What happened to your training? To all that time I fucking wasted on you.

She felt as if she were shooting through a million-mile tunnel. Stop, she bellowed. Stop threatening me.

He gasped then retreated a few feet. Threaten? he yelled. Are you insane?

You hit me in there, she cried. That's what happened.

His eyes rolled upward briefly, all whites. Then he handled her aside and staggered to the boat's railing, wrestled a set of doubles out of the way so he could lean over the water as if he might spew.

Am I right? she called after him.

He turned painstakingly on the railing and over-slung his rear. Don't get me started on what your fourth screw-up was, he said. What you did. Get it? What you did to yourself. Your little freak-out in there. So this is the last word I'll say on the subject. Wake. The fuck. Up.

What were you trying to do? she said, horning in. Kill me?

He lifted his huge head. Blank-faced now, he gripped the railing and leaned backward away from her over the water—so far she thought he might let go. But then he pitched forward and opened and closed his mouth a few times. Me? he finally choked out. You almost killed yourself. On this piece-of-shit wreck. Which I'm only diving because of you. Because you needed the practice inside. Remember that? I should never have let you talk me into another trust-me.

The sun flashed from behind the cloud and she shielded her eyes. Good, she said. Because obviously I can't trust you.

He squinted into the glare and dragged a thumb across his forehead. Don't blame me for your fucking problems, he told her. And don't think you're ever fucking diving with me again. So don't worry about trust. You're on your own, dear.

You think I need you? she said.

Gulls mewed behind his back. He scrubbed the top of his head with his hand. Oh, he said after a moment. Glad you got that off your chest. Case fucking closed then.

That's right, she said.

He shifted towards the water again and spat then faced her once more. I thought you were dead, he told her, seeking her gaze. You know? Dead?

She corkscrewed and peeled off her hood, whapped it in the direction of her stuff and stalked into the cabin. Blinding dark after the brightness on deck. Crazy quiet, everyone bummed. Before her eyes could adjust, she banged into a series of knees which swung from her like gates springing open. She located an unclaimed morsel of bench and, still standing, crammed her thighs against it for balance as the tug rocked. She yanked the zipper on her suit and ripped hanks of hair as she worked the neoprene seal over her

head. Her bladder was a sack of molten lead. But pissing would mean making her way in front of everyone to the bucket stored beneath the wheelhouse and
nobody did that—these mopes just wagged their dicks
over the side of the boat. And Iron Jane, in here too
somewhere letting her best fucking friend stew, this
unfaithful, ungrateful friend somehow just held it, as
Marilyn usually did. Fuck's sake. Still semi-suited, she
lurched again, again knocked knees—Jane's included
probably, Marilyn could only hope as she headed back
to the door. Just as she reached it Rand plowed in,
nearly knocking her off her feet. Fuck, he shouted,
and righted her quickly by grasping her shoulders and
firmly settling her in place as if setting a post. Then he
vapoured around her and melted into the huddle.

Now the small granite islands in the distance looked
like giant doorknobs. If a giant hand turned them they'd
open onto what lay below, a place that seemed to suck
at her now as she alone kept watch over the diminishing
wind and the moiré pattern etched onto the increasing
surface calm. Late in the day. An orange glow in the far
distance. Soon twilight would grizzle the sky and fall
like rain. Darkness would settle before the boat reached
the southerly shore of the larger of the islands where
the lodge lay. And the room she unfortunately shared
with her husband. Right beside it her perfect, perfectly
thankless friend's room—if it hadn't been for Marilyn,
taking up diving, for once leading the way, Jane wouldn't
even be here, she thought now. She fixed her sights on
the horizon's blazing slash, its leaping line of fire.

14

Unreal, unfair.

She arrived late to breakfast the following morning, scavenging the only remaining chair—beside Rand—at the round table in the lodge's cramped dining room. Forks clanked but otherwise the men quietly fixated on their handsets. The half-eaten toast in front of her must have been Jane's.

Marilyn imagined her friend now on the docked boat's deck. Organizing, cleaning, restoring worn-out gear. Reviewing her dive log. Marilyn flinched. Not a word from Jane yesterday as they'd debarked, no quick shoulder pat or sympathetic murmur. Marilyn had marched on her own like a mechanical toy to the cabin where she'd holed up wrapped in a blanket on the couch while the others ate. She snagged her fingers now on her dirty curls. Rand scrupulously ignored her as he dispatched his eggs. She slumped further in her seat, recalling Jane riding shotgun in his truck several days ago on the three-plus-hour drive north from the city—Jane unleashing the seatbelt and leaning forward at one point so Marilyn could rub the tight muscles in her friend's back. The two of them gorging on walnut crullers at some rinky-dink town's Dairy Daughter. On the car ferry to the island Jane had looped her pale hair into a topknot and Marilyn pulled her wool beanie on and together they'd braved the ferry's upper deck for the two windy hours so Marilyn could fight her motion sickness while Rand cozied in the lounge with a coffee and crossword. On the deck Marilyn and Jane talked work—a project launched, a proposed grant. They discussed plans for a little dive time together, the next day on the wreck—a tune-up for Marilyn but a challenge for Jane—but also eventually more ambitious dives too. Maybe next year or the year after when they both, as Marilyn charitably put it, had more downtime under their belts. Just not this trip. Not with the season drawing to a close. Not with her eagerness to notch another big one. Of course, Jane had said. Why sure.

And when they'd arrived at the lodge Marilyn hadn't felt ill at all. She and Jane had clinked beers over that first night's bonfire. Her vinegar-honey scent had prickled Marilyn's nose when they hugged fiercely before bed.

Let's kill it out there tomorrow, Jane had said, eyes shining with excitement. But Marilyn only gave a wry smile.

Someone passed Marilyn a mug. The thin liquid scorched her mouth. She recoiled, sloshing coffee and soaking the leftover toast. Rand swung his head in her direction and grimaced. Sorry, she hissed, thinking mostly of her friend's arms around her. She felt weak, robbed. Self-robbed—her ego had prevented her from partnering with Jane the whole trip instead of turning to her husband, who now was setting to work pulverizing a bacon strip.

The great Rand. The sway he held here. Across the table a ruddy-cheeked duo Marilyn sort of knew jointly refused to acknowledge her. Beside the taller of the two, Jason—compact and brown-skinned with close-cropped hair—grinned sheepishly at her before quickly cutting his eyes again at his hand-held. He was a meticulous guy, dedicated to training one small step at a time. Read up on every journal and discussion board. Was his previous regard for her on mute? Next to him was Matt, a shaggy ginger, precise where it counted, which at this moment entailed accurately measuring the waffle-to-egg ratio on his fork. He dependably crewed for Leo, the boat's skipper, a smooth duck in his late twenties with silky, elegantly tousled fair hair. He was also scrolling through his handset, and only picking at his food.

She wondered if she should try to eat. She swigged her cooling coffee. She listened to people chew. Her stomach turned.

When Rand pushed back from the table everyone glanced up. He resettled in his chair, bumping her arm.

Sorry, she hissed again.

He cocked his head at Leo. There a plan? he said.

Her apology last night also hadn't flown. He'd returned to the room late, undressed and showered and collapsed into bed. She remained on the sofa while a rising wind conked the trees outside. With any luck the whole rocky island would bust. What hadn't she already lost, including her recent pride? She'd encountered a frightened fish or Rand's overkill knock—what did it matter? In her panic she'd forgotten the drill. All there was to know. The cabin's eaves creaked. He tossed in bed. Hours passed. I'm sorry, she finally said. Go to sleep, he snapped. *Dead. I thought you were dead. You know?* For the rest of the night she replayed his words. She did know. The terror and guilt of outliving. The sensation of falling out of life's rotation into some cruel limbo. The pickled dread of what might come next—more dull life and then more. He'd lost his parents to a car wreck when he was a baby, too young for him to recall. But he did remember close friends who died while cave- and wreck-diving—men and women he'd sometimes name after lovemaking, his fingers afloat in her hair, chuckling at old, once-shared jokes. Instead of twisting alone in his own private versions of hell while she stewed in hers on the sofa. Did he sleep at all? When grey light soaked the edges of the drawn curtains she scuttled to dreamlessness like a slick pool. And when, drained and exhausted, she opened her eyes again, he'd already left.

Leo coughed, squared his shoulders and puffed his chest. He rapped his knuckles on the table. Okay, he announced. Here's the situation. Marine forecast says twelve knots out of the northwest by ten. That's a lot of rock and roll. I can get you freaks out there, but I doubt you can get down. Or get your sorry asses back on board.

Rand stared at him and she followed suit, noting as she often did Leo's peculiarly elfin nose and jawline, the skin strangely unsullied by sun or windburn from the six or seven times a season she and Rand chartered his services. A leather bracelet and a chunky steel-banded dive watch adorned his slender wrists—the watch expensive-looking and impressive only to non-initiates since technical divers relied on computers. Now, under Rand's steadfast gaze, Leo's shoulders caved slightly. Okay, he said. So *you* can get down and back. But what about these pussies here?

Jason and Matt and rest of the guys snickered. Matt flipped Leo off. Pussies? one of the guys said. Bro, that is so unfair.

With a snicker Leo gave a wave of his long tapered fingers in her direction. Sorry Mare, he said. Don't mind me. I'm just a pig.

Rand stretched then got to his feet. His acne scars had taken on a grey cast. Purple crescents rimmed his eyes. No rare blue today. We're on, he said.

No please, she responded to Leo. Don't mind *me*.

As if anyone was. Someone knocked her chair getting by and then someone else did. Guys. Guys in the morning. She could almost sniff the testosterone. Probably they'd all drown. Even Jane. Even her husband clearly not at his best, who couldn't find it within himself to disappoint anyone, except his wife. Someone should stop them, insist they sit this one out. Not leave her stranded with the greasy dishes and crusts streaked with jam, tea-party leftovers from a social event held in honour of an imaginary friend invented by some suck.

15

Blown out. There really was no sailing the tug in such snotty weather. By late morning everybody packed and left. For much of the miserable ride to the mainland on the car ferry, Jane and Rand occupied the lounge, plying crosswords while Marilyn scanned the shabby receding vista from the stern's upper observation deck. The trees on the island's shoreline looked like puny sticks—this late in October, this far north, on vegetation not terminally acid-rained, the dressy leaves had long since turned to mulch. Another two months and the water's surface would congeal. By December the ferry would yield to snowmobiles and cars and trucks racing to fishing huts stacked with cases of beer and fishing poles angling lines under the ice. She'd seen that cold underworld for herself once. Slipped on a cold sunny February day through an opening chainsawed from the twenty-inch crust into water unperturbed by surface disturbances and found a junked car on the bottom in such crystalline relief she expected it might start up and drive off. Just past its rear bumper she noted a motionless pike carceral with cold, eyes clouded with winter dreaming. Its grinning needle-sharp mouth. She wasn't under long though— not nearly long enough. Secured by a rope to a topside line tender to prevent her from getting lost, a nervous, jumpy guy who insisted on cutting short her allotted time by yanking feverishly every two minutes on her harness, she'd returned to the hole feeling like a dog on a leash —until, just before she exited through the hole, a near-hallucinatory blue at the ice's underbelly elated her. Those memories still held their goodness, she thought now on the ferry's deck, holding onto herself, again shaking with cold. Some memories still might.

She paced past the towering wheelhouse. She imagined the captain or pilot or mates watching her walking, wondering at how tortured she must look. How desperate to escape. But with no one visible behind the mirror-like windows, the wheelhouse looked like an impenetrable fortress. She glared. She could almost believe there was no one up there. Nobody home. Not even a ghost.

The ferry continued its churn over wrecked schooners and stunted white fish. Partway through the crossing— increasingly frigid and splattered, the sky dehiscing sleet like grey seeds—she tried not to watch a sparrow, spastic in the slurry wind. It seemed desperate to alight, likely having followed the vessel too far from land. Finally it spiralled into a dust-up of feathers and foam.

Three days later she woke pinned to the mattress. Nine in the morning. How late. Her husband's big head on her belly. He brushed his lips against her navel and gently massaged her hip. For two nights he'd slept downstairs on the couch. For two days and nights she'd mostly lain stricken upstairs in the bedroom of their tower-tall townhouse in a smart old-new mixed district across the river from her scuffed former place. Now— no thanks to her, to anything she'd done to change his mind—she located her legs and arms, slowly gathered her other parts enough to make love. After, she wiped a smudge of sweat from his neck. I missed you, he said.

Yes? she peeped—and then she dozed and then woke to him pulling on pants and selecting a shirt from his closet, his shoulder blades so sharp she marvelled they didn't cut his skin. She half expected his knobby spine to rattle. She wondered at his sudden weight loss. She wondered if she should worry about his worry over her. Over them. She marshaled her remaining strength and sat up. I miss you already, she called as if across some vast gulf.

She felt like an insect whose head had been severed from its body but whose legs kept soldiering on. Apparently still going. To the bathroom, for instance. She stared at the beady eyes staring from the medicine-cabinet mirror and worried a comb through the gnarled garlands of hair. Then she dressed and creaked into the hall. So late. The townhouse seemed to echo as she crept down the steep stairs. An inky blip and she was on the second floor already, in the kitchen. Fridge, stovetop. Her stomach rumbled. She opened the fridge and located the juice and set the carton on the counter. She heard something moving in the walls. She ignored it. And then, as if it were the most ordinary thing in the world, she removed the frying pan from a cupboard. The stove's gas control clicked and the pilot light caught. Here she was. Famished—beyond belief, she discovered, composing and consuming a killer omelette. Extra pieces of toast. Finished, she licked the crumbs—delicious, like sawdust—from her plate and disposed of it in the garbage container then stood before the stainless sink and admired the spackle of eggshell. She worked the faucet and water gushed. Here were her hands equipped with their marvel of skin and nail. So she was still covered. Safe.

Work—messages returned and new ones sent, appointments reshuffled, amends made, fingers crossed. The morning streamed by in her first-floor office. She hummed tunelessly, head bent to her tasks, pleased at the absence of the usual ear-achy vertigo and leaky sounds that followed a dive trip.

Mid-afternoon she hopped in her car and gassed up at the nearest gas station and then headed out, wheeling the wheel beneath sugar-dust clouds. Bright summery fall—as if she'd only imagined the cruel northern weather of the past weekend. Or it existed in a past so ancient she could discount it. In no time she was travelling the cemetery's drive. First time in months. She swept beneath the chartreuse and saffron and fire-opal leaves of sycamore and hickory, elm, maple. She soon stood before the double plot. Marilyn Wolfe, begat of Wolfes—what the cancer and subway bomb had left behind. In her mother's case, what the years of starvation topped by medical treatments had wrought. As for Marilyn's father, what the private search organization she had hired was able to retrieve from among the rendered fragments, enough at least to hold a proper funeral. Now she rattled the small, customary stones in her hand. She was of a long line of sensitive, flinching people, survivors begat of one of history's more exigent planned enterprises—a thousand-year-plus genocidal ingenuity of mass graves and incinerations that in her mind took on the shape of the cloud of starlings, too large and dark for her to fully apprehend, that murmured the otherwise clear sky before settling to call and cry in the nearby stand of pines. Sole child. Last in line. Almost gone herself. However strange she might feel at the moment, who was she to throw herself away? And with herself, the turquoise ring lost at age nine. At thirteen, the misplaced dragonfly-shaped notebook containing her sketches of weeds and wasps and also a taped-in scab from Jane's fabulously distressed, bike-accident-prone shins. Even her mother's middle-aged late-night Ativan clamouring in the living room armchair outside Marilyn's teenager bedroom. You dirty little, you daddy's little. Even her father's crack at her jaw one evening outside an ice cream shop when she didn't walk as quickly as he wanted. Spoiler, spiteful, her parents sometimes labelled her. Mom, Dad! Dead but not gone, not when Marilyn still dreamed them alive, meeting her on a subway platform or in a department-store shoe department. Looking good. Like your new hat.

No, she thought now in the cemetery. She'd had her close call. Now she had her work cut out for her. Up here she'd protect what she still could.

And so thinking she stared into the shiny granite marker at the shrunken, dry-eyed figure until a series of black saccades shredded her vision—and when they cleared, a faint memory scraped to life and she squeaked into motion and placed her quartz nuggets on top of the headstone. Bird-ee a bird called and a chipmunk wrestled a pinecone by a rose bush. But beneath her feet the dead remained dead. Let them, she thought. Let the dead go on doing their dead things. She herself was here. Barely here. And that was enough. Enough! She touched her cold fingertips to her eyelids. Black branches wheeled like cold constellations and her ears rang. No one answered. Meanwhile she would work and work and pay her respects here and here only and day would follow day and she would with all due respect follow her days to a far-off end.

Then it was December and really so beautiful, so unseasonably warm. For weeks the silver maple outside her office curled its branches prettily like lashes and the wet breeze batted them. One whole half-day she watched from her window as a hawk, one wing dangling at an odd angle, perched in the honey locust. Most days she texted her husband and he texted her back. She combed through her curls and long strands curled on her desk and December turned wetter then clear. Then the days grew longer. April arrived. The people two doors down in the tower of a townhouse identical to her and Rand's, the couple with the peach tree they'd planted in organic soil and never pesticided, these people had the peach tree cut down and a parking pad put in the tree's place. Marilyn combed and combed her hair though sometimes her curls pulled back, defiant, and some of her hair fell out. She viewed such drama—there for all of her to see, though who was watching the watcher? she wondered—on the drawing pad and once she even drew around her hair irregularly shaped moles related to a work project. Dot dot. Dash dot dash. Dots like pom-poms. Dots, snow, birds. She saw them everywhere. Dot dot dash dash, dots jouncing into the air, skirting the ceiling and flashing through the windowpane, clear through. Her ears rang. Outside, a blue sky. Its screen of dot dot dash. Then she left her desk to fix a nice lunch and drink and after, all business, cross-sectioned the dangerous moles and pressed send. She read the news. Yesterday another explosion. She napped. She woke and her head ached. She ate again, ate the way a mere mortal might, hungry all the time! Little wonder. How else honour a mother who'd died curved-fingernail thin. A father who'd told her mother not to eat so much. Father in bits. Dots and dashes.

Another April arrived. Wait, Marilyn told it. Nuh-uh, nope. You most certainly do not.

PART THREE

16

She held court as if the waterfront diner were a lavish chamber beyond which lay opulent vistas. She pronounced on an expensive procedure touted in certain doctors'-office magazines, and a new restaurant in New Downtown where the chef conjured abalone foam on dry-ice chips. The phantom sensation of motion from the previous afternoon on the bay—the boat's fast gloss over blue water—presented like silk slipping repeatedly from her skin. Never mind the sunburn. The itching and bloat. The greasy early breakfast so she could steal time with her friend who in an hour or less would suit up. Down to some sticky underworld she'd go with Rand, already at the underwater-cave site tweaking gear. Some treasure—Jane sullen, coughing and breathing wetly over her soggy pancakes. When she glanced at her handset for only the fifth time Marilyn dropped all pretense. Done? she grunted.

All yours, Jane said and lifted the stringy hair off her neck and let it drop. Go crazy, she said.

Nearly a year had passed since Marilyn had given up diving, but she could still remember the business of trying to force food into the hair-trigger gut. She wound a finger through the syrup pooling on Jane's plate and tasted it—an unravelling sweetness gone almost before she knew it.

You done? Jane asked.

Marilyn's scarfed eggs reappeared like scalding liquid in her chest. Queasy, she considered her choices. Offer advice and admonition and come off pissy-jealous. Or better—stash Jane under the motel-room bedcovers and crank the death-metal AC, crack one of the bottles of decent vintage Marilyn had bought at a city boutique before driving up on her own a day later than Rand and Jane. Marilyn chewed the inside of her cheek while men in colourful shorts and women in pastel capris and flips straggled into the diner. Like them, she was a tourist now. You go ahead, she told Jane. It's on me.

Jane shoved to her feet. There was a downward list to her chapped lips. You sure? she said.

You're not still here, are you? Carry fucking on.

Nothing to do now but watch Jane's back, her rigid upper torso and driving strides. See you? You too? The diner's screen door flapped open and shut and rattled the picture windows bleached with glare. She squinted. Outside, a family with fishing poles claimed the white-washed dock. On the rocky shore below two kids wagged their guppy bodies and barked like little generals, haughty with desperate joy on the last long weekend of summer vacation. She knew what it was like—the ruthless effort to make the most of what was left. She fumbled at the plates in front of her. Semi-blinded by sunspots, she nested the melon-slice garnishes, inhaled the deepening, ascending scent of musk and ylang-ylang. She called for the bill and paid. On the dusty road she groped in her shoulder bag and clapped her oversized sunglasses into place. She felt terrible, stretched and distorted as if her insides were too large for her skin. For a moment she hung back in the diner's oasis shadows. Terrible. Time to kill.

17

Nearly noon. Starving. Sole customer on the rooftop deck of the bar, she doused her chicken strips with malt vinegar and set to work on the near-year's worth of padding between her bones and the yearnings her now-gone slenderness once yielded. She crossed and uncrossed her legs. Her sunburnt skin chafed against the wooden bench as she surveyed the marina's scruffy local tugs and polished yachts up from the borders for the precious early fall colours. She sipped her beer. Metal clanked on the street below and she ignored it to flick at the meticulous cloisonné of a ladybug decorating the napkin draped across her spreading thighs. More clanking. Gas hissed and her ears shrilled. She leaned over the railing next to her bench and peered down at the street. Leo. He sprang into the bed of his flashy white truck and shut the leaking valve, his lanky hind-side poking out of his jeans. As if she hadn't had her fill of him yesterday on his boat. But his dive shop was only three storefronts of caps and maple fudge past the bar—everything in this town was close to everything else. He shifted and exposed his dirty-blond soul patch new to her since she'd retired herself from diving, and in marked contrast to what must be his bottle-born light-blond mane. On the boat yesterday, she'd had little to do but study Leo alternately blustering and lazing while Jane and Rand reviewed maps of their cave. Little to do, like now.

Another tank shrieked. You cunting slut, Leo yelled at no one in particular.

More beer. She decided that when she finished she'd order another. Below her Leo reached with his sinewy arms for the offending cylinder and then straightened, slim-hipped and wide-shouldered, in Rand's weathered Bend-A-Friend tee—what all the other wannabes wouldn't give for one. It was a limited edition doled out at a cave-diving conference in the south attended by the usual elites. Like Rand—who literally gave Leo the sweaty cheapo shirt off his back when he'd fussed over it, pestering like an undeserving brat. She recalled that they'd been on a ride back from some northern dive site—some dive she herself had nailed, unlike Leo, she consoled herself by thinking now. But Leo fronted complimentary air fills and cookouts and boat trips. In exchange Rand adopted a shut-up, put-up arrangement. Something else she knew about, she thought, observing the glister of fat on her chicken until her appetite deserted her. She wished she were home, at her desk graphing stoma and denta divorced from anyone she'd ever met. She pressed the tines of her fork into her palm. She wished for canker and boil. For septicemia. For any rash undoing of the body in what used to seem to her—before her near-death in the wreck, before her parents' deaths—an adventuresome unfolding, lush and wild although mostly these days she just worked grim and grimmer. But better that than playing tag-a-long. Guilting Jane. Wishing she could guilt Rand.

She took another pull on her drink and ignored the sharp mix of voices from the street. Light flared a few feet above her—sun banking off a circling gull. More voices. Leo was climbing from his truck. A few of his guys milled about while he pirouetted in the road, chest thrust forward. He'd always struck her as tightly strung, jittery and high-handed. She pegged him as a premature ejaculator—needy and pushy and unable to hold himself back and therefore not much fun to tease, perspiring overly onto the sheets. Even so she balled her paper napkin in her lap and plastered on a smile. Beggars can't be choosers, her mother used to tell her.

She called from her belvedere. Much ado about nothing, Captain?

He shaded his eyes with both hands and looked up. Who's that? he said.

Forgot me already? Marilyn?

He lowered his arms. Shit, he said loudly to his mini-militia. Gets worse, don't it.

She considered tossing her glass but really she wished for thunderbolts, then more reasonably for bulbous tumours or raisin-sized nodes. Any kind of flesh-wreck. Special delivery, Leo. Even so she took a few seconds to rehearse her next line. What's that? she finally trilled. Didn't catch you.

He cupped his hands around his mouth. Something's wrong, he bugled. Someone's missing.

Sunlight ignited his hair. A burnt tang seared her nostrils. Her head rolled.

When she came to she was on her feet. Amber streamed onto the decking and she stepped out of its wake and righted the glass. Garble roiled her mouth. She wondered how long she'd been gone.

That's all I know, Leo shouted, then his silhouette moved shiftily around as if facing a disagreeable decision. Yeah, he said after a moment. You'd better come too.

18

She crowded between Leo and some Tim or other in the heat-stink of the truck's cab. Leo slammed it onto the two-lane highway, the tanks racketing in back. The leaves crimped red on the stupid trees clumped like leftovers on the stony abandoned farmland to either side of the road. She swam her tongue dumbly in her mouth. Leo soon slowed onto a dirt road that quickly yielded to tire tracks rutted into burnt grass. The tracks ended at the fringes of a wood and the men clambered out and padded around Rand's shiny black ark of a trailer, his dreadnought-black truck. Here too were his portable compressor and booster pump—when running they shrieked and clobbered like an army of pneumatic drills in a child's nightmare—and a pyramid of tanks stacked beneath a tent awning that also sheltered a workbench arrayed with toolkits and spare hoses. Tim cut an admiring whistle—apparently unlike Leo he'd never been to this mostly secret site.

A sudden breeze beat open a small gap at the edge of the woods and then the gap quickly shut—the trail. It lay several miles inland from the huge bay on one side, the great lake on the other, veining the narrow peninsula and leading directly to the cave. She scrambled now from the truck only to fold at the waist and nearly puke. The scrappy grass turned black then white. She straightened and wiped her dusty mouth on her wrist. Even the sky looked X-rayed. Even Rand's stuff and Jane's—her small extra suit airing next to his large one on a picnic table and her tool kit tucked neatly under the bench. Marilyn's mind shuffled these and other stark details. So much to go wrong—sometimes she woke in the middle of the night with a wall of water in her face, cold sweat brining her skin. She'd reach for Rand, the cascade effect of fear—the body's soaring, plunging chemical transactions—mimicking the old lust. But after—as he dryly kissed her and settled on his side of the bed— she'd feel only her own pulse tapping in her fingertips as if trying to get out. Sometimes even the sex failed.

The sky seemed to clamp over her now like a lid. Leo and his guy kept at their busy buzz and she involuntarily swatted the air. And then with a minor roar another truck jounced along the rutted tracks. Soon a cop cruiser and SUV appeared from behind the truck's hovering cloud of dust and Leo and crew commenced waving, self-important as politicians. True—someone had called Leo instead of her. Wife, best friend. Her mind rumbled and she fought to take stock. Someone had called. Someone was missing. I'm going, she announced.

Leo and Tim stared as if they'd never seen her before.

She floundered ahead along the footpath and entered the forest, descending a nursery-tale thicket of evergreens, dark stippled with peeling-parchment grays. Cool must wadded her lungs. A few minutes and she arrived at the rim of the four-foot-wide gash in the ground—a twelve-foot-deep vertical cleft with a small aluminum ladder attached to one side. Two hand-helds lay beside the hole. Gagging at the sulfur stench, she recalled her last time here this past spring on a whirl-wind, one-day surprise visit to clumsily help Jane and Rand suit up. Marilyn had peered from this exact spot and felt the seeping chill on her bare arms. *Bon voyage,* she'd called down. *Don't do anything I wouldn't do.* And, watching first Jane then Rand at the bottom of the sink squeeze beneath a limestone ledge, had thought: *no fucking way.* By their accounts no cave Marilyn had ever toured was as cramped and murky and cold as this one. So thank you and fuck you two too, she'd thought as her friend and husband pressed past fanged cracks and into boa-tight rooms formed over eons by underground rivers carving rock. They'd plumbed rough mineral shafts with their lights while their breath-exhaust percolated around them—Marilyn knew all about it, or once knew, or knew enough, never having entered this too-bruising system herself. She'd then spent hours beside herself, lungs rilling, unable to catch her breath. When Jane and Rand had re-emerged and unsuited and debriefed, laughing and chattering, Marilyn had word-lessly stood around. Alone, lost. *Dummy,* after a time she'd knee-jerked into her car and veered precipitously home to take her place among arterial mazes and veinous routes like the avenues and crooked alleys of an old water-buried city.

Now a bulky shape began to crab from underneath the ledge. A whimper escaped her. She lost her footing and woodchips pressed into her knees. A huge black suit, a monstrosity of gear, laboured up the ladder. His back to her. Of course it was him. A blizzard of white moths stuttered in her brain.

When he was level with the top of the sinkhole he ponderously swung around and pushed the heavy, bottom-mounted battery pack for his primary light out of the way and sat, flashlight-spiked helmet still on. Face still masked. Lips swollen. A few seconds passed before she sprang forward. She released straps and unclipped his suit's intake valve, the steel bolts and brass snaps stiff and hard to work. She removed the back-up regulator snagged by the choker of surgical tubing he wore around his neck. He tore a glove off with his teeth and juddered his tanks impatiently and she dodged to keep from being knocked down the hole. He worked off the other glove and ripped at the strap to his helmet and tore it off, then twisted the mask around from his face so that it perched eerily backward. He hunched over and hacked. Get me more fucking air, he finally shouted into his belly. Now, so fucking help me.

She launched at him again and grabbed his shoulders and he wrenched away, pressed a thumb to the side of his nose and blew. Snot sprayed and she swiped at her cheek. She felt a crackling in her chest. No, she told him. I'll go. I can use Jane's extra suit and gear.

Groaning, he clapped his hands over his ears as if he might pop off his head.

Something flashed in her vision then died and she dropped again to her knees. Okay, she said. But listen to me. Did you even decompress? You've done enough. More than enough. Let someone else.

There is no someone else, he roared.

19

Too soon the rim of the sinkhole teemed with inaction. She tottered above the foul-smelling cleft while beside her two non-experts wiped sweat from over-heating faces nearly the same lurid orange as their latex dry-suits—the kind that tore easily, that no real technical diver would ever sport. To their credit the cop divers seemed aware of the extent of their uselessness, having jettisoned the rest of their crappy gear at Rand's base camp. They evidently weren't happy though. Shit, said one of them a few times. Yup and yup, said the other. Then the first one said, Serves her right. And Tweedle-Dee said, Yup, chick was asking for it.

Hey, assholes? she said. Who's asking you?

The melting orange popsicles seemed to melt more. Apologies, they mumbled.

The other cops came in two varieties, standard uni-form with vests bulging under sweat-stained shirts, and plainclothes wielding notepads and badges semaphored from wallets. She answered to the latter though their effortful expressions said it—impossible to really explain the situation. After a while they merely appraised her as did Leo and his few other cronies who now rounded out the flurry of activity at the site. She did her best to hide the old rage she felt resurfacing from when her father died in the subway bombing and media crews shoved cameras and microphones in her face and she received calls and texts from producers. How do you feel? How do you feel? they all wanted to know. And Marilyn had only wanted to scream, Feel? Feel?

She drifted now toward the treeline, as far from the sink as she could get without leaving altogether. She stood alone, chopped some patchy grass with her heel, watched the men back until one of the cops arched his brows at her and checked his old-school watch. You bastard. Acid cut her throat. But then with a sudden heartless gobble she filled her lungs. Here, alive. Fuck yes. Then the elation passed and her skin fumed with sunburn and shame. Her mind continued to chug. The moment the air ran out, she thought. The moments before, trapped and too late and knowing it. Sickened, she clenched and unclenched her jaw. What else? She knew roughly how long the air in Rand's fresh set of doubles would probably last. And Jane's air?

When she quit diving Marilyn ceased to dream her parents alive at a kiosk on the platform of a subway station or in a hospital room engulfed in radiant white. No more second chances. No more dream-kindnesses to offer—a cup of water for her bedridden mother or an I love you! for her father lettered in fastidious script and tucked into his pocket and fondly rummaged for in the seconds before the blast. No more hope of setting in motion again the dead. Of waking crazed with the marvellous feeling of having been—gladly, joyously, with such release—sawn in two.

Finally Leo retrieved her. Marilyn? he said carefully and loudly as if to a child. Let's get Gerry to take you back to the motel.

Gerry? But she let Leo tuck her under his armpit and roll her like a suitcase onto the path to the base camp and some Gerry or other as advertised—the Tim-guy she'd ridden next to on the way here. Leo cranked open the door to his truck. Here we go now, he said, sidling his hands to her hips.

Wait, she said.

Leo's pretty face, inches from hers, blanked. Don't, he told her, his voice very low.

What time *is* it? she said.

Leo looked as if he might cry. Don't cry, she thought. Then shouts busted out and she fled.

20

He'd settled on a large rock near the sinkhole. Stripped of his tanks, he shed his muddy hood and unfolded his neck seal, breathing exaggeratedly as if to mime that he could. With each exhalation he appeared smaller—a few more and he might vanish. Unless she stared hard enough, sucked the fact of him in, nothing but him, investigated his every sinew and nerve, cupped him inside her, somehow sheltered and possessed him and him alone.

How could she? Several men were hoisting Jane's black-clad body from the sink. At the top they slabbed it on the dirt. Marilyn winced and then remembered— she was the one who easily bruised. Someone cut off Jane's hood and slit her seals. Released, her good skin seemed to pale by the second—no sign of yesterday's sunburn. Strands of her wan hair curled like seahorses. Jane and not Jane. Not the desperate pregnant woman on a windswept street corner one afternoon thirteen years ago, scared defiant, abandoned by some guy, shouting, Call me you bitch. Abandoned by the very same bitch. Abandoned this morning too when despite Jane's evident anxiety Marilyn did nothing. Don't go, she might have said. Keep safe, I mean it. She could have warned Jane about the obsessive pride and rough lessons that bordered too closely on the fatal. Fatal—what did that even mean? The not-Jane here now? Who'd stood in for Marilyn, taken her place in diving. And in death?

Another bleating, euphoric second overcame her—still here, I'm here. And then Rand lurched from his rock and lumbered over and lowered himself to the ground next to Jane. He cradled her face in his palms and his facial scars seemed to distort and worm like living things. He rose and it was Marilyn's turn. Menace, bitch. She dropped and mashed her lips to cold lips. She slithered her tongue, probing the cool mouth, snagging a chip on the lower front tooth, trying madly to flick the uvula, tiny bell. Calling and calling. *You* bitch. And shouldn't someone be applying CPR? Until a doctor arrived and pronounced? She blew and blew, hisses and sparks. Her head whirled like a spangled top. She had sequins for eyes, a terrible glitter.

The spell broke when someone tugged her upright and crooked her to his side. Sorry, Leo said, as if sorry were for him to say.

Sheer fucked-upness. Perched again on his rock Rand wept. A cop photographer snapped pictures of the body and site. Someone—Rand—would at some point have to retrieve Jane's equipment from the cave. He'd apparently left it inside to make the recovery easier but her gear would also require documenting and analyzing. From her parents' deaths, Marilyn knew the after-life as another hell of details. There'd be an autopsy. Maybe an inquest. The photographer clicked and clicked and nearby the two cop divers slouched. These hotshots like to play their games, one of the spitting images said, rubbing the long-weekend stubble on his blunt mug. Yup, said his lookalike, lowering his voice to a fake-sounding baritone as if he were reading a script for a much older and wiser man. And we're the ones that have to clean up, he said.

Leo tightened his grip on her. She considered yelling, shoving, switching him for Rand. But he was crouched next to his rock, puking for real.

The photographer said, What're these Lone Rangers trying to prove anyway?

Beats me why some people do what they do, one of the orange glows said.

21

She waited at Rand's base camp, propped on the work-bench under the awning while he gave his statement. She clenched and unclenched her toes—her sneakers felt too small, as if her bones were spreading yolk, as if some-one had picked her up and dropped her. She wanted to leave. Leo was holding forth with several guys over by the parked vehicles and she waved experimentally to see if she could catch his attention. Get him to take her away, back, somewhere. After a moment she gave up. The shade under the awning deepened. If only she could vanish—lose herself like some dummy sidekick. Except then she'd feel even more alone. She sank her head to her knees. Within seconds, it seemed, Leo rematerialized, his arm around her shoulders. A mole winked on his neck. His breath on her face was like chicory crossed with car-nations, a smell chemical and latent. But at last her wait was over. Into the day's furnace with her. Then into his white truck which ferried her through the dust and gravel to an enchantment of empty blacktop. He drove fast and silent. An oncoming motorcycle whined by like a mosquito on steroids. A minivan glissed into sight then swept alongside and seemed to hover briefly before passing— Leo thought she was staring across at him. I don't envy you, he said. Finding out like this.

She nodded. The breeze sifted the needles on a stand of spindly pine. A tourist trading post then a gas station emerged by the side of the road—tricks, she thought. Ruses to convince her the truck wasn't rolling in place while the surround peeled like rind. More beguilements when Leo banged a right into the motel parking lot. The grounds appeared devoid of vegetation. The single-story cinderblock structure, topped by a low-slung roof and with one filmed-over window like a newt eye peering dimly from each of its seven rooms, created an effect of dormancy. It was as if the place were rooted below ground and hadn't taken yet. He parked next to her car and rested his hands near the hillock where his jeans rose over his crotch. You want I can go in with you, he said.

She let herself from the pickup and slammed the door. Her image blotted its shiny surface and then the truck revved out of the lot, taking her reflection with it.

She entered the room. Double bed with threadbare coverlet and knotty-pine walls. A clutch of nickels and pennies on the dresser. Yesterday's underclothes heaped on the floor in a study of conjugal squalor. On the other side of the flimsy wall, Jane's room. Marilyn crumpled onto the bed and rummaged in her mind as if through a toolbox—she needed to call Jane's family, say the right thing. But only a sprawl of scaffolding and ingeniously placed mirrors appeared. She curled onto her side. Last night she'd played her part well, had taken no small role in broadcasting an ardent thwucking of the headboard against the panelling. As if to say, Here lies the passionate duo. What lies, she thought now. Sweat pushed above her upper lip and she licked at it. She felt as if she'd been rushing for days and weeks and years and now the rushing had stopped.

Miraculously, she slept. Merciful blackness. And woke to Rand hunching through the door. I know, he was saying into his handset. Thanks, me too, I can hardly believe. Yeah, she did. Drained them. Fuck yeah. To the last breath.

Then he was off the phone and right back on again with a similar script as he paced the floor. She got up. She folded her clothes and in the bathroom zipped her toiletries case. She got it—the elites drew together to protect against the know-nothings who might close off sites and shutter shops dealing in services for the technical sort. She understood too the need to exhort and extol, to tell each other they were very sorry but look how brave their endeavor was, to not quit now. What might she contribute to all this? she wondered. I'm glad you're safe, Rand. Sorry now? Sorry as I am? While she had questions for Rand, the questions she had for herself were larger. She closed the bathroom curtains. She peed and flushed and cried into a towel. She flushed again and splashed water on her face then slit open the door. No, he said. Another passage, a new one. No idea how far back it goes.

She clicked the door shut again and knocked her forehead against the wood until black spots rashed her vision. When she finally re-emerged he was quiet, lying on the bed. Tears leaked from his eyes. After a moment he spared her a glance—all it took for her to go to him. Though his embrace was limp, she was grateful enough to hate herself. She clung to him for a moment. Then she bungled from the room, bashed her bags in the back seat of the car and jammed the key in the ignition, her self-loathing a wizened pea that kept shifting and irritating but also soothed since it was hers, all hers. At least something was.

22

She veered onto the highway and shot past the flyspeck town and then the two police cruisers stationed at the turn-off to Rand's base camp. The late sun burrowed in the side window and heated half her face. Poor farmland unscrolled. She passed the Dairy Daughter, the Hi-Style Donuts. Jane had dubbed much of the drive scenery-lite. What, Marilyn wondered, was the scene of Jane's final escape? It escaped Marilyn. She could only picture dense and mud-stuffed. She wanted to imagine just one open passage and tug as if it were a thread and have Jane tug back. Marilyn wanted the skipping rope they'd bound each other with as cowgirls and astronauts roaming the Allen family's dishevelled backyard—Roger that, got a Red Planet dust storm moving in, keep together, don't lose track—to bind still. But she had lost track. Her fault. She'd let Jane go this morning. Let her get taken up with Rand and diving in the first place. Unbound, bawling, Marilyn gassed the car hard. She took a hand off the wheel and rummaged a tissue from the coin tray. She felt woozy, smudged as if stupid with sex. She removed her other hand from the wheel and knuckled the growing bump on her forehead. A horn blared and she grabbed the wheel again and swerved, tasting metal, blood from her bitten lip, soiled breath.

She stopped for coffee and a chocolate bar. Huge clouds massed in the darkening sky. On the road again she passed a farmhouse with a hand-lettered sign in front. FLOWERS 4 SALE. U PICK. She swung around at the first turn-off and parked on the dirt drive. She climbed the wooden porch steps and knocked on the screen door while something, a loose shingle maybe, beat on the roof. There was a slow clopping from beyond the door and then a tinkle of unseen chimes and a middle-aged woman appeared behind the screen. She emitted a few asthmatic noises and her face, blurred by the wire mesh, appeared gaunt and streaked with imperfectly applied foundation and blush. Full auburn bob that might be a wig. A faded pink jersey outfit sacked around her frame. Marilyn understood she was staring. The flowers? she stammered and the woman punched her lips together pow-pow and disappeared back into the house. The shingle, if that's what it was, tapped like a shoe and finally the screen scritched open an inch. Knobby fingers extended a pair of scissors. Marilyn accepted them. A single swollen digit pointed to her far left.

Past the maples and oak, giant gladioli grew in stiff waves that rendered visible the heady wind. The clouds were bolting and she knelt in the fluxing light. Though the scissors were dull, green liquor soon stained her hands. Dummy. She'd fucked and re-fucked her husband as if sewing a needle through fabric, concealing her doubts—about him, herself, diving, Jane diving, what they were all doing, what were they doing?—like excess fabric, pleats in a skirt. Idiot. She worked her borrowed scissors until she had her bunch—red and coral and white with stamens brushed with saffron and a few buds that hadn't opened yet. The sky had slowly turned a bruised blue and burnished gold and she seethed at the radiance, as unreachable as Jane. Marilyn would violate her now if she could—prise her best friend open so she could question her, pound the sense back into her, the Jane bunkered tight now as an oyster, lips cyanotic as a winter violet, an aragonite luster at the corner of a closed eye, a single tear like a milky sac.

Her own eyes stung. The air felt grimy, particulate with twittering bats, like a time-travelling echolocation of Jane's scoffing laughter and riot-act readings when Marilyn needed them post-parents' deaths. And those teenhood dare-scares—requiring Marilyn to scream strings of suck-mes at some gangly dude ambling past their table in the high-school cafeteria one lunch period. Jane jeering and throwing her own head back mouth agape, gasp-laughing—only to stop laughing and lean forward clutching Marilyn's arm. Dead serious? Jane had said. That as far as you can go?

Streaks of furious sorrow splayed inside Marilyn now like forked lightning. She dropped the flowers. They lay on the ground like fuses of colour. She wanted to grind and ignite them somehow with her heel. But the sky crushed against her and she crouched once more and snatched up the stalks. She imagined their withering trajectory even as she dandled them.

23

Home. She hit the remote in two places at once and the gate swung, the garage door revved. She nosed the car in and parked and turned the engine off. The door slung down behind her and she rested in the plush quiet—and again woke, this time feeling misshapen, stiff. A struggle to warp from the car and flatten past her husband's storage containers and gas bottles, to open and close the townhouse's inner door. The alarm system chimed and she disarmed it then tapped on the lights and unlatched the shuttered closet containing the mechanicals and engaged the AC. For a second, the irregular patterns on the hallway's slate floor eddied then stilled. Then she slogged past her office and climbed the tower-steep stairs. Dazzle of clean counters. Double oven perfect for multi-course feast-making though she and Rand mostly used it for fancy frozens. She dislodged a glass from a cabinet and stocked it with ice. The ice sizzled and popped and she held the tumbler to her sore forehead then exhumed her handset from her bag. Exhaustion grew in her like weeds and she felt winched open, exposed, a rustling inside her like scurrying rats. What to say! She tried to recall when she'd last spoken with Jane's dad but failed. Marilyn set her device on the counter and swizzled the ice with her finger then ran it along her gums until she felt them shrink. She felt like something chalked on a sidewalk, all outline. Once more her ears rang. Call. Call. The fridge's motor sounded like a zipper opening and closing at high speed.

Coward. In the darkened bedroom she dropped fully clothed onto the bed. She panted into dreaming then choked on and off into consciousness. A car parked on the street outside. Jane-y, Marilyn heard. She heard, Mare-i-lyn—in Mrs. Allen's soprano some distance from the root cellar where the girls once shushed each other among sacks of potatoes and onions. Medallions of spider webs swagged the low ceiling—it took buckets of bravery to get here but now the girls were outside plucking poisonous berries from the Allens' hedge. Fake slurping and belching, the girls slipped into the shade of the lion-maned elm. Girls! Come out, come out, wherever you are. Mrs. Allen's voice grew louder, closer. The girls thrilled at hiding in plain sight.

You're going to catch. it, Jane suddenly crowed, pointing at some spatter on Marilyn's sneaks.

Dripping red.

She gasped. Her pulse staggered and leapt. In her hypnagogic toppling, wind stropped her ears and she toppled off a cliff.

You awake? Rand said. Mare?

High above, the ceiling was a floating socket. On the edge of the bed sat her husband, furred with wriggling dark curlicues. He smelled sour, sharp like scallions. Don't shut me out, he said. Please.

She coiled upright. In the corners of the room tessellations appeared—crowns of antlers, dark nests with their shadow treasures, all that once flocked to her deep in the freezing back chambers of flooded mines and far inside caves and wrecks, narcosis' brood. With each the dire need to check her gages every minute to remind herself where and who she was, recall how she'd return in one piece. A miracle, it seemed to her now, that each time she'd made it back.

He thumped the wall over the headboard with his fist. Talk to me. You think it's my fault? That I put a gun to her?

No, she said.

He stretched onto the mattress and she felt his corrugated breaths. Do you wish it had been me? he said.

Her stomach rumbled, or his did. How unfair their bodies with their idiot needs. How their bodies went and went. If he was guilty, she thought, so was she. She snapped on her bedside light. He flung an arm over his eyes.

Do you wish it had been me? she said.

Marilyn, he said after a silence. We're all we have.

24

Sunlight bladed through the blinds. The sheets felt oily slick. He lay sprawled carelessly as litter across his side of the bed and part of hers. Littermate. Her uncovered bare legs seemed to stretch far from the rest of her. Across the room, paint strokes wavered unevenly where the walls met and a watermark she'd never noticed before oozed. He stirred and the sheets seemed to foam. Her peripheral vision flanged—an occlusion then a flare. The wall stain fluxed and she fixed on the dresser and then the windowsill as if fighting seasickness. He sighed in his sleep and she remembered. Last night, bestride her, he'd wiped her lips with his glans, pre-ejaculatory liquid seeping from his urethra, his testicles high and tight. She'd opened to him and he fucked her face like a drawer slamming repeatedly. Then they'd arked at their trunks, torsos rearing. Pure humping. They were all each other had. Until an image of Jane bobbed like an apple in Marilyn's vision. She howled and clawed. Mistaking her efforts, he pinned her hips and came, then fell into a fast slumber still inside her. She slept too, awoke in the night with his dick shrunken and slipped from her.

The wooden floor beneath her feet with its boards in even strips steadied her now. Full morning. He began to snore and she backed from the room.

Jane. Wide-spaced eyes and pale wheat-coloured brows. Two days ago, a girl soon to be stolen to darkness, she'd reclined in a summer meadow on an island called Flowerpot, her teeth picking around the pit of a plum—the single piece of fruit she'd agreed to eat from the robust picnic supplied by her friend while Rand and Leo post-lunch dipped in the bay. I know it's exciting, Marilyn could have said then. You're all caught up but maybe you should slow down, take things one step at a time. And then Marilyn could have suffered Jane's hall-of-mirrors retort. Like you did? Because isn't the danger the attraction? The attraction, the danger? Which is exactly when Marilyn might have just said, Stay the fuck away from my husband.

Descending the townhouse stairs, she squeezed the railing as if she might wring moisture from it. Two days ago on that island Jane's eyes had shone like ball bearings. She was, Marilyn thought now, a woman not yet stolen. But already called.

She took refuge in her office with its shelves arranged with boxes of computer programs and manuals and colour swatches, stacks of spiral-bound drawing pads. Her multi-screen workstation was ornamented only with a framed photograph of her and Rand on a boat, formally attired in their tuxedo-black drysuits. The happy couple.

I spoke to them, he said from the doorway.

Hey you, wait for me, Marilyn had called to Jane two days ago—they'd finished eating, the tasteless remains of costly cheese and bread and chocolate for Marilyn, the plum for Jane, who was striding up the rocky hill away from the shore where in the distance Rand and Leo basked like walrus-lords. Her toned calves bulged and her sandals smacked the bottoms of her small strong feet, her butt swished athletically. Wait up, Marilyn had called, struggling to keep pace. Wait for me.

I can't hear you, Jane had yodelled and kept on.

I told them you were too upset to talk, he said, advancing toward Marilyn in her chair. She turned her back but his fingers were cold and unearthly as starfish at the nape of her neck. If you can manage to go, he said, it would mean a lot.

Go? she said, picturing Jane walking briskly along the hill's crest to ramp, intact, down the other side and out of view while Marilyn remained here, breaking apart.

His thumb and forefinger pincered slightly then released. To the Allens, he said. They've asked us. This afternoon with just the family. It might help you too, both of us.

Help? she said.

Finally she had her mission. She gathered clothes and laid them on the bed, tucked panties inside pants and bra inside shirt. Her creation seemed to regard her. You putting me on? Then, while her husband stalwartly manned his phone in the living room, she slathered her face with make-up to conceal her self-inflicted bruise from the motel's bathroom door.

Outside, clear as ether. Her car sliced with a metal-glide ease through the Sunday morning of the long weekend's mostly vacant avenues and lightly staffed checkpoints. In Old Downtown she hung left and left among the glittering multiplexes and into the relative darkness of a mostly vacant car park where she ascended a series of elevated rings. The flowers she'd picked yesterday emitted a fetid scent from the back seat. After parking she stashed them in a trash can near the elevator. Then down she went and outside again onto the bright street with its glossy surfaces and gadgets behind every storefront. Searching, searching. She leaned into a narrow alley between the closed establishments and puked a white froth in a mechanical uh-uh-uh. And then she was climbing back into her car. A package lay on her lap, a pretty cardboard box wedged between her gut and the wheel. She opened it, dimly recalling glazed pastries looped in rows like glistening pods behind display glass. An old-fashioned cash register's ping. Now, in the car, she poked then tore off a chunk of crust then scooped and gulped leaving only a single staring berry, a salt-sweet mineral-tart, stuck to the foil pan.

25

Randall, Malcolm said, and Rand entered the Edwardian row house, shutting the screen door in her face. She clutched the fancy replacement pie closer and took in the veranda dishevelled with dirty running shoes and rain boots and trikes, rolled-up umbrellas, a broken wooden chair she considered collapsing into in hopes of splinters spiking her too-tight skirt, of blood-letting and pain loss—if only. Instead she let herself into the small dark hallway congested with toys and winter coats hanging from hooks and quickly negotiated the too-quick passage into the living room with its tribunal of silent Allens—each so pale as to appear powdered. Mr. and Mrs. Allen senior on the loveseat. Malcolm—Jane's brother, eldest of the three siblings—by the brick fireplace and Jane's older sister Amy hulking on an ottoman with three tots around her knees. Fair-haired to a person, but Jane had been fairest of them all. Not one of the Allens seemed to notice Marilyn. She chewed the inside of her cheek and shifted from foot to foot, feeling like a spare hour on a clock. Where was Rand? If only she could announce herself or some news, an important development, impart an understanding. Prick herself awake. Growing up, she'd envied Jane for having a large family. She could disappear into the crowd. Many times Marilyn had sought refuge from her parents' scrutiny in the Allens' living room while the TV blared and the kids sniped over which channel and how many saltines per. She'd blissfully burrow in with her sketchpad. Now she stood outside Malcolm's living room, desperately wanting and not wanting to break in, to look and not look each of the Allens in the eye. To act.

Hello? she muttered.

Heads cocked. Like dolls, it shamed her to think.

Marilyn, you must be beside yourself, a voice called from the dining room.

Malcolm's wife Katie raced to Marilyn's side and wrested the box from her hands. She shot a glance at Malcolm. He pursed his lips and gazed at the floor.

Yes, I imagine so, Marilyn said.

Mr. Allen senior removed his glasses. He was portly and it took him a moment to locate his pant pocket and withdraw a hankie. Mrs. Allen quivering beside him, he cleared his throat. Marilyn, he said. Please know that you are in our prayers.

And you in mine? She couldn't get the words out. Thank you, she said.

Rand appeared in the entryway to the adjacent dining room, balancing a cup of tea. We just can't believe it, he said. Please know we are so very, very sorry. Heartbroken.

Strangled sobs emerged from Mrs. Allen senior. Malcolm flattened his lips. Amy reddened. Rand, she said huskily. Thank you for calling first. Letting us know before the police did. That's a blessing.

Yes, he said. We were sure you'd want that. It was the least we could do.

Heat festered in Marilyn. We? Where she'd failed, Rand had made good and contacted the family—even before returning to the motel. Her shame deepened.

What will it be, Marilyn? Malcolm said evenly, as if she were on some inconsequential visit. Tea, he said. Apple juice. There might be wine. Milk? Water.

The football-playing meat of his high-school days had softened and thickened. She'd noted it maybe six years ago at Amy's second wedding, but the effects were considerably pronounced now. Marilyn? he said.

Wine please, she responded—in fact she could feel it already, thick slugs of it down her throat.

He frowned, nodded. Wine, he repeated—and with a sigh made off, Katie and pie and Rand in tow.

Tittering erupted from one of Amy's brood. She roughly patted the child from her ottoman throne until he rocked from her reach. Eyes sparkling, he clapped his hands over his mouth and jerked his shoulders side to side as if playing a game. Mummy, he piped through his tiny fingers. Mummy, what did the lady say?

Amy dragged him onto her lap and bounced her knees. Stop it this instant, she said in a low voice. Or Mummy will slap you.

His face froze. The other two children's mouths kinked downward as if they might cry. Marilyn edged toward the vacant lounger and sat. The children, she recalled, were from different fathers. Amy's third marriage had endured six months. Her first two husbands had been married to other women when Amy trampled onto their scenes. No love lost either between Amy and Jane. Newly full-hipped and rampantly bosomed, deliberative, Amy had once mermaided around the shallow end of Memorial public swimming pool one July afternoon, snapping the elastic on the bathing trunks of Jane's first boyfriend. Within the hour Amy and beau were taking turns lapping from a can of grape soda and crudely necking on the walk home while Jane and Marilyn trailed behind.

Amy trained her scowl on Marilyn now. We're not keeping you, I hope, Amy said.

No, of course not, Marilyn said.

Go now, Amy said, and shooed the kids toward the dining room, the better to fix her attention on Marilyn. *You* don't still dive, do you? Amy said.

Packed it in last year.

So you were the smart one after all. Funny how that worked out.

Marilyn tensed, recalling Amy's big-sister knees jabbed into the soft undersides of arms, fists to guts. Headaches that lasted days and stupendous bruises. Worse, there had been Marilyn's mother's bath-time prying. What the hell did you get into this time? she'd exclaim. What's wrong with you?

Kidlife, Marilyn thought now. A miracle she and Jane had survived it.

Not smart, Marilyn gently remonstrated. More like not brave enough.

Amy puffed up on her seat. Brave? she rasped. Some brave.

Mr. Allen roused himself. Amy, he said, his thick glasses magnifying his watery eyes. Please, he said firmly.

More like pure selfishness, Amy continued anyway, voice rising. Trashed what God gave her. Threw her own life away for no reason. As if it was really hers to begin with.

Mrs. Allen's weeping freshened and Mr. Allen put his arm around her. You may stop right there, he told Amy.

Why didn't *she* stop? Amy said, then she pointed at Marilyn. Or why didn't *she* stop her?

Mrs. Allen quieted herself now. I'm so sorry, she said to Marilyn in a dampened voice. You must excuse us.

I should give you some time alone, Marilyn said, standing, stupid with anguish. Excuse *me*. Please.

Bowls of grapes and pretzels bedecked the dining table. Where was her pie? It alarmed her how much her mouth watered. She turned to face the intense scrutiny of a row of five coin-eyed sprites perched on chairs pushed against the dining room wall, Malcolm's kids having joined their cousins. None of them were eating. Her stomach rumbled again and she wondered if it would be rude of her to snack. Suddenly the largest child kicked his legs and caught Marilyn's calf. Excuse me? she protested, straightening her spine in an attempt to loom large.

He shrank from her with a scared expression. Your wine? Malcolm said from behind her.

She wheeled as if caught. Then she took the glass from him and, trying not to notice the stern, quizzical look on his face, sipped her drink too quickly, coughed and nearly spilled it.

He drew back as if she were something he'd stubbed his toe on. Need anything else? he said and indicated her glass. More?

She tossed the rest of the wine down her gullet. Pointing the glass in front of her like a torch, she followed it into the kitchen.

Rand and Katie sipped tea at a counter jumbled with notebooks and pencil cases. There too, in the centre of the mess, lay Marilyn's untouched pie. What was wrong with it? She felt an unearned, rankling sense of injustice. So many feelings, she thought, and nowhere to put them. For example, her distaste right now toward Katie, Katie communing and commiserating with Rand. I wish we'd been able to reach her, she was saying. She needed help. For most of her life, from what I'm told. Keeping herself apart so much. A cry for attention, really. When it was family who could have helped her most.

If I'd known, Rand said. I'm so sorry. If only.

He seemed unaware of Marilyn's presence. But Katie glanced over her shoulder and stared. You need to stop, Katie continued to him. Take this as your sign. If you do, her death won't have been in vain.

His shoulders heaved. Marilyn watched in helpless horror as Katie gathered his head to her breast. His back chugged up and down. From behind, it almost appeared to Marilyn as if Katie were breastfeeding him. There, she cooed, not breaking eye contact with Marilyn over his shoulder. There, there.

She twitched from the kitchen. Small mercy—no sign of the children in the dining room. She edged her wine glass onto the table and yanked at her skirt, which she now noticed had ridden askew along her thighs. Could she just leave now? On her own? Would that be the worst thing she'd ever done?

Hello again, Marilyn, Malcolm called from the living room. More to drink?

She adjusted the somehow turned-under collar on her blouse. I really should get Rand, she declared with more force than she'd intended.

Katie! Malcolm boomed. Fetch Rand, would you? Time to deliver him back to his wife.

26

She connected a few until he managed to snatch her wrists. You're hurting me, she protested.

He loosened his grip. Blood trickled from his lower lip. What do you think you're doing to me? he said.

Her car baked. Along Malcolm's street of brick mostly-rehabs, leaves hung like rags from the trees. Rand began to weep as he had this morning before his shower and after, while trying to decide what to wear. His good suit? Save it for the service, she'd advised. Plashes fell now on his khakis and soon she pitted her wet sounds against his. Finally he let her go—so she took another swing but he ducked and she banged the dash. What am I doing to you? she shouted. Who cares about you?

A woman studiously averted her gaze as she walked a dog past the car. A sprinkler came on of its own accord on the small lawn next to Malcolm's. Marilyn, Rand pleaded after a moment. You know she died doing what she loved best.

I do know, Marilyn spat at him. But you sure seemed to be saying something else in there. To your new best pal, Katie. So you shut the fuck up.

I had to say something, he said. Somebody had to.

Marilyn went for him again, slapping the air, his headrest, his botched face. She gave up when he stopped dodging. It's okay, he wheezed. It's okay, whatever you need to do.

She concentrated on the breeze fizzling the tree branches. After a while he stopped crying. She stopped. The woman with the dog walked by in the opposite direction. Malcolm came onto his porch and peered out at the car then went back inside.

She did not do herself in, Marilyn said. Tell me I'm right.

Rand clasped her hand and she let him. I'm still trying to figure it out, he said. Looks like she cracked a valve.

What about her back-up?

The whole manifold seemed off. Cops have her rig for testing so we'll know for sure soon. I hope. Fuck what a mess.

A mess, Marilyn agreed. Better to throw in with him than the terribly grieving Allens whose understanding, as far as she could tell—terrible to think this of the family at such a time—misunderstood the Jane-ness of Jane. As if in agreement, the sun winked white off the spokes of the parked bike next door to Malcolm's. And what about the tail-flash on that streaky afternoon-sluggish sparrow there by the curb? Bright things. A sharp flicker everywhere, if only Marilyn knew where to look. She turned the key in the ignition.

It's me, Rand said. I've fucking gone and lost another one. Maybe Katie was right. Time to stop.

No, Marilyn told him, releasing the brake. No, she said again, rolling the word like a polished stone in her mouth.

His thinness scared her. Like a sack of bones, he seemed a jumble she couldn't add up. Until she could, if she worked hard enough at it. Sit up straight, she wanted to tell him.

No? he said, bearing an expression of terror and surprise.

27

She popped another breath mint then entered the humid church. The lozenge seared her stomach and gummed her mouth as if a sticky cocoon nested there. Too much Scotch the night before. Too much wine before the Scotch. She processed past sweating limestone walls alongside her husband as a foggy choiring issued from the church gallery to float beneath the vaulted stone ceiling. Rise up my love, my fair one, and come away. She nodded at a few of Jane's aunts and uncles and cousins and several workplace friends and colleagues, including Nina and Martin, Jane's co-directors at the agency. Marilyn knew them all, from various get-togethers, but not well. Jane had lived other lives, Marilyn knew, and the thought now webbed her head blind.

Rand steered her to a glossy pew in one of the first rows and they sat. A woman in front turned to them with a tight smile. Not Jane. Marilyn cast a backward glance, then more carefully scanned to her left and right. Not a single

Jane here, the one Marilyn did know. No girl in a blue robe and white wimple performing St. Mary at a Christmas pageant Marilyn herself attended as a guest of another faith—a title with which the priests addressed her afterward in the church basement where Marilyn and the Allen siblings helped serve tea. Though what had faith been to Marilyn growing up but the *Shma* recited before bed until she was eight years old? Or the Hanukkah latkes percolating in a fryer? Nothing, not a sliver beside her faith in Jane and her ability to plunge ahead and her seeming faith that Marilyn would follow not far behind a girl who swept off her wimple to pick scabbed knees or who, at sixteen, back-and-forthed tequila behind the high-school portables before first-period English. Who lifted purple eyeliner from drugstore shelves and co-contemplated doing a fuck-ton of boys in the Ottobar's bathroom stall—and sundry other ordinary pastimes of girls and almost-still-girls with limited resources striving to invent themselves with what lay close at hand, ridiculous boys and petty crimes and misdemeanors, but striving nonetheless. Who as women fished through the labyrinthine aquifer of underwater caves and the hidden interiors of shipwrecks, pushing back the darkness of the unknown—of themselves too, of what they could do. This Jane. And for a time this Marilyn.

Rise up my love. My fair one. Come away.

It was glorious, this moment. Her brain nearly shrieked with it. She felt wonderful, astonished, at once repellent and ascendant. Jane was dead. Dead! If still believing in Jane wasn't faith, what was?

In a corner of the church basement someone's blazered sleeve caught her saucer, and tea washed over the lip of the cup. She tracked her husband as he conversed by the coat rack with fellow condolencers. She shrank further into her corner. Then came Amy.

Forgive me, she blared, expression contorted.

Please, Marilyn said, startled. There's no need.

Amy's legs nearly straddled Marilyn's. There is, Amy said.

A whiff like insecticide—Marilyn's own alcohol-mint breath on the rebound? Forgive me? Marilyn said.

Amy's face grew heavy, relaxed into sadness. She reached out and touched one of Marilyn's curls. Stay in touch, Amy said. Don't be a stranger. Like she was.

Ass-fucking hypocrites.

Vintage teenage Jane. On her hands and knees on the neighbour's patio, upchucking while Marilyn braced her from behind. They'd been babysitting and, having delivered their charges to bed, had quickly bellied up to a line of Jell-O shooters on the kitchen counter.

Your family advocates anal sex?

Outside on the grass Jane had lurched to her feet. Precisely, she said. Through the back door if you have to, but remain a blessed virgin until your Mr. Prince shows.

Fearing the snitch-neighbours, Marilyn and Jane hadn't exactly hollered to fuck Mr. Prince, fuck him up good. But drunk as could be they'd laughed so hard in each other's arms that they'd eaten each other's hair. Summer gnats hovered over them like tiny souls.

In her living room she cracked a fresh bottle and poured another sloppy one.

Jane had never actually said, Your mom is crazy mean and your dad flirts with me too much. Marilyn had never actually said, Your parents don't care how smart you are, they think good grades make you stand out too much, make you pray less, might scare off the Great Charming One.

She slammed her drink. Rise the fuck up. She felt terrible, ugly. Blaming the Allens. Blaming her own parents. Rand. Might as well lock herself in a box. Sloshed, she tucked her legs under her on the couch. Good times. Middle of a weekday, Rand at work while she fell behind on her own projects. Outside the living-room window her street commenced its goosestep through the mad season of mid-September, a cold-hot march before the leaves on the trees detonated with final colour, sacrificing themselves to the ground. She examined her drained glass. *Salut* stranger. Arise too Marmalade and Panda, Jane's family cats batting a crippled mouse between them on the kitchen linoleum. The old neighbourhood creek swollen with snow-melt—back in the years when winter meant heaps of snow. Arise even the two young women parting on a busy sidewalk on a watery, windy day in spring. Call me you bitch. Marilyn would take even that back in a second. Even the one whole summer when she and Jane were nine and spirited a rusty trowel from Mr. Allen's rickety toolshed to cut small disks of grass from the Allens' backyard and bury treasures beneath the lilac bushes—a gnawed-on ballpoint pen found by the side of the road, scraps of paper with single words written on them, Hi! Ribbet! then carefully folded over, an inexpensive earring pilfered at scorching risk from Amy's dollar-store jewelry box. Marilyn and

Jane carefully concealed their handiwork, resetting the browned parcel of sod so it reknit into the woof and warp of magic-carpet rides over a vast cave of wonders they whispered about on frequent sleepovers.

Marilyn set her tumbler on the coffee table and stood and hitched her pants. Rise up now. Please. Come the fuck away.

Fuck. She toddled down the stairs. Past her neglected office to the front door she went. She put her ear to it. Footsteps clipped along the sidewalk beyond the wrought-iron gate. Surely no one she knew. Or wanted to know. No one searching for her lost in her ridiculous tower of a townhouse. No Jane to the rescue—all this time Marilyn hadn't realized how much Jane needed saving, needed Marilyn's help. Jane, Jane, Marilyn thought anyway. She peered through the peephole but it was like looking through a fun-house distortion—zippy cars in candy colours and tidy shrubs and pert birds dispersing for somewhere better. Who knew where? Who cared. It made no sense to think but she thought if she could sleep some more it might help. Apparently she'd forgotten how. Or she needed more something-anything but she'd forgotten what. Something before her very eyes she couldn't yet see.

She lay on the bed. Drifting. The sky waxed to a blue-black filling her window. Way out and beyond, stars coursed the night's channels like an overlay of light and motion both there and not, laws inscrutable, anarchic. She recalled a time when she lay on her stomach in the submerged mouth of a river cave with some heavy current of crystalline water blowing past. She'd pulled some major deco, so a very nice narcosis was blowing her brain. Zoning, she gazed at the gravelly bottom. Suddenly, two pebbles detached themselves from the beige surround and looked at her. The freshwater flounder was slightly smaller than her bare hand. She reached out and tapped near it. The little fish lifted. Anything could happen. She tapped some more in a semi-circle around her and fish after fish rose like tiny perfect puffs of smoke. See you. You too.

PART FOUR

28

Twenty-three hours in the truck hauling the trailer south down the continent. They took turns piloting through flotillas of space-station-sized rigs to the tune of all-night-radio crazies, caught pee breaks at service centres the size of towns.

When they arrived it was dark. A shower would be good. But first they swung into a small lot and strolled to the river. The air vegetal and thick, the moon full. Two owls screeched at each other through the moss-bearded cypress and pine. Standing on the high bank she couldn't tell where water began, it was that clear. Like transparent air though less so when the polluted vernal run-offs mucked the aquifer. At least the water still existed. There was that. Still clear for now in fall. She thought if she could shock to stillness the bass and mullet and gar schooling below, she'd be able to count each overlapping scale. Clarity. A hundred million gallons a day gushed from the three spring caves here—Little Devil and Devil's Ear and

Devil's Eye—that lay beneath the surface. Intending to scoop some of the water, she clambered a few steps down a short ladder that descended to the basin, but mistaking one element for another she soaked her foot. Deception. She'd forgotten. Been away too long. Rand and the owls hooted at her.

Several weeks before, in what already felt like another time in a faraway land, she read the updated online fatality list. She read the forums.

HOW I WANT 2 GO.

FAREWELL, TRAVELLER, DIVE ON IN THE BEAUTIFUL AFTERWORLD.

BYE DUMB BITCH, PUTTING YOUR LIFE IN HELL ON PURPOSE EARNED YOU A BODY BAG.

YOU SHOULD LIVE SO WELL, TO DIE DOING WHAT U LOVE.

She stopped reading and dug her gear from storage and cleaned and treated it, prising apart and adjusting as she might illustrate the effects of toxoplasmosis on the nervous system or the five organ-ravaging stages of an infectious disease so new it bore only a sequence of numerals for a name. Mother's ding-dong cancer lung. Father's liver and left-earlobe in shreds. The beauty and terrors of the body! She reassembled her kit instead of meeting deadlines. Some bankable projects Marilyn refused outright, bestowing on others in the grisly trade. She had a little saved, she reasoned. She could afford to let things slide on the work front.

One day she borrowed Rand's pickup and carted her tanks to a fill station to have them inspected and pumped. Then she drove two hours to an abandoned water-filled quarry where forty feet beneath the surface she searched for the busted school bus a local dive club had gutted and sunk.

Found it. She tied some line to the passenger-side mirror then ran the reel in the front door and through the murky centre aisle to the back row. She tied the other end of her reel to a jutting metal strip. She removed her mask. Blind, she followed the line out, bumped down the steps on her hands and knees. Outside, she donned her mask again and reversed course, continuing to make contact with her thread since inside now was solid murk from her clumsy disturbing of the silt—might as well still have her mask off. Working by touch she then recouped her reel. Then, still inside, in the back of the bus, she reached behind her neck and turned off first one and then the other of her tank valves. Three sucks at her reg. A resisting fourth. Then the choke-hold of no-air. She opened her valves and reeled out of the bus. Practice makes perfect. She farted around in the shallow depths, daisy chains of perch and sunfish petalling around her. She fiddled with back-up lights under the cool gaze of a four-footer pike and ferreted the old set of decompression tables stored in her waist pouch. Her computers, bulked one to a wrist, blinked green. She worked her way around that bathtub of a place, drilling and two days later did it all again—priming, practicing. Leaping, it felt like, but in a series of controlled movements that seemed the opposite of reckless. Seemed right. Which she knew couldn't be true, making a wrong right—okay! a shit-pail of wrongs—but still she kept on.

Leaping, one night she got into it with Rand. It's too early, he said. Wait until next fall. We'll go nice and easy at first. Belize or Truk this winter.

No, she told him. You go nice and easy. If that's what you want. I'll go ahead on my my own.

They were in the bedroom. She lay sprawled on her stomach, chin on one hand, TV remote in the other, surfing the channels, sound low. Almost everything was commercials. Gone mute and crushed to one side of the lounger, he stared at the screen. What happened to Jane in the cave remained unknown and both Marilyn and Rand had declined to discuss it. What was the point, for now? The coroner's report could take months. Flip flip. She found a sitcom and stuck with it.

She endured her soaked sneaker until she and Rand got to Bruce Bowman's double-wide on the heavily wooded grounds of the springs. That's quite the mind-fuck you had, Bowman said, grinning as he greeted her at the door. Don't worry, won't hold it against you. This time.

Even from Bowman's sticky living-room couch she could detect the river smell. It spored, she imagined, through the door and window screens, straining past the moths that pressed to the mesh, seeking the interior light. Aw-shucksy Bowman nodded at her from his lounger, stroking a tabby on his lap, and though she inwardly cursed Rand for showering first and abandoning her, she feigned a genial interest in the cats and more cats occupying Bowman's place—black, white, black and white, tortoiseshell and more tabbies under the desk pushed to the trailer's window and under the bookshelves and on the chairs opposite the couch. They obscured her wet footprints on the sorry-excuse shag and paced esses on the coffee table, leaving snake impressions where their tails dragged along the two bottles of beer Bowman had plunked down. A sleek tawny suddenly flung itself at her and colonized her lap with tiny claw pricks. Youch, she said, shifting the animal about to minimize the damage.

So, Bowman said. Been awhile, Marilyn. Remind me?

Spooky Bowman. With his chubby face and stocky build, fluffy light-brown curls threaded with silver and portentous bags under his eyes, he seemed like an aging cherub. She guessed he was only in his late thirties and not the forties or even fifty that he seemed—his kind of diving tended to prematurely weather the few who managed it. Some of his pushes were legendary, and his glazed eyes—mark of the ten-thousand-logged-dives diver, permanently nitrogen-saturated and codeine-enhanced, eternally mildly stoned—betrayed an inward-looking sheen, as if he were attuned to some interior mechanism. Cagey Bowman. She recalled how he always gave the impression of taking in more than he expressed. He scooped the cat now from his lap and carefully set it on the floor. Then he grabbed his beer and waved it at her. Come on Marilyn, he wheedled.

She could smell her own sweat. She'd done her training on these very grounds, with Rand had visited Bowman's personal lair half a dozen times. The old feeling of being scrutinzed and judged here hung over her still. Maybe a year? she said.

He widened his eyes. Right, he said, stretching the word out as if in disbelief.

The cat in her lap stretched and purred. Hello kitty, she said, palming the animal's vibrating throat. She picked up a paw. It was wide and flat and the cat curled its eight toes around her fingers. She'd forgotten. Bowman and his collection of polydactyls. This one's pretty friendly, she said.

He was smiling and not smiling. She is, he said. That's why I'm keeping her. The others I waste.

He tipped his head and laughed then raised the bottle to his mouth and glugged. Before he'd retired early to cave-binge and scare the tourists he'd been a silk-suit on the investment market. At least a dozen years later he apparently still relished playing the role of redneck hick to the hilt. He put the beer back on the coffee table and, squinting, held his arms in front of him as if sighting along a rifle. He singled out a ribby feline by the floor lamp. Pow, he went. Sometimes my breeding program goes squirrelly. I use the mutants for target practice.

Smart kitty, Marilyn said.

Yeah, Bowman drawled. *Oh* yeah.

She picked the cat off her lap and deposited it on the floor. She nudged it away and plucked up her beer. Sip and shut it. She wondered how much Bowman knew about the accident. All Rand's phone calls in the aftermath—most likely some were with guru Bowman, long-time pal who looked right now as if he were trying to stifle a sneeze. Or a laugh. Fine, she thought. Let him. She just drank and listened for the shower to stop.

Rand emerged wearing clean khakis, his long toes gripping the weedy shag. A cat immediately began rubbing his calves. Sorry Mare, he said. Hot water ran out.

Honey, Bowman said before she could reply. Sorry *honey*. Get it straight, Petrie.

She rose fast. I'm good, she said. Think I'll call it a night though.

Sure? Rand said warily.

Bowman snorted. Petrie, buddy, he said. Didn't you hear the news? The lady says she's *good*.

Full-cheeked, snub-nosed. Broad-chested with a pudge-rimmed stomach showing beneath his tight-fitting tee. A comic book, pale-skinned, iron-man baby. Larval. A textbook label sprang to mind. Neotenous.

Fuck you, Bowman, Rand said. Where the fuck's *my* beer?

Thanks, Bruce, she said, and shuffled a few feet toward the guest room, then turned for another look.

He hoisted his bottle as if toasting her. Why no, Marilyn, he said. Thank *you*.

29

She woke late. To her relief Bowman was gone. She had her shower while Rand made coffee then carried their mugs into the leafy outside. In the filigreed shade sequined with cat eyes she and Rand unhooked the trailer and stocked the back of the pickup with what they needed for the day. They drove to the nearby air-fill station where they helped each other lug their doubles then they hit the road for real. Leaping, her stomach in knots. The live oaks and pines by the side of the road seemed prickly as barbed wire. Soon they parked on a dirt pull-off and got out. Flies and mosquitoes buzzed and stung. She scuffled through her prep and, squeezing her head through her drysuit's tight neck seal, experienced sudden vertigo—claustrophobia's flip side. She fought the flailing urge to belly down on the ground. Unfit. Fucked. She should call the dive. Forget it.

Might as well bury herself. She folded the neoprene flap on her seal and zipped. I'm good, she told herself.

Fine, thanks! Rand slid a hand toward her, a praying man-
tis perched on his finger. Hello there! she chirped, and it
rotated its green-cube head in her direction. She wondered
how she might appear, J-pegged into its dimension.

And then the weight of her rig seemed to drive her
along the dirt footpath and onto a wooden platform
and down a ladder to the spring. The water had a green-
ish-brown tinge in which gray particulate appeared like
oversized dandruff—far less current charged this spring
system than the one she observed last night, and less
roaring discharge meant greater impurity but also an
easier swim in and out. Also the cave was relatively shallow and she knew the site from previous dives. Given
her rustiness, good for me, she thought as she flippered
the surface to the far side and peered in. Disarticulated
tree roots. Scabby suckerfish and bushy algal blooms.
And a gash in the bank's outcropping of limestone—
another deception. Entrance to a Karst netherworld of
conduits and drains. And yet so much more than mere
plumbing—million-millennium-old passages carved
by water. Rock beds for fossilized trilobites and ammo-
nites—the earliest cave explorers—and relative-young-
ster mastodons, and the even more youthful Arawaks,
the region's extinct indigenous peoples. Sightless and
translucent living arthropods and fish flicked among
the fossils like the dead's dreams. When overviewed on
a map, the various passages—explored and surveyed by
divers like Rand and Bowman—appeared dendritic, as
if the cave were itself a neural system, a rock-creature
alive in its own ancient mineral time older than wars
and sex and beheadings over inaugurations and rights of

return and every niggling Am I right? As she waited for her husband on the water's surface, dangling above the cave opening, she felt like small bait.

Finally he showed. He hefted down the ladder and, in a few strokes, reached her. He immediately vented the air from his wings and dropped. Old times. She plunged after him only to wait on the muddy bottom as he tied line from his main reel to a thigh-sized root. Then he ran the line inside and down. Inside and down she went. Catfish trolled the cave's large vestibule. She and Rand turned on their primary beams and swam farther in. Where daylight yielded to twilight he clipped his reel to the previously installed permanent line. Okay? he signalled. Okay. From here she led beyond all natural light. Not swimming—flying, shedding the vertical inclination of the species, the usual upright terrestrial posture. Her respiration deepened as if honeyed. Despite her suit she felt denuded, skin-sloughed. Alert-minded. Loosed into a tunnel fifty-five feet below the surface and thirty feet in diameter. Buff-coloured walls, deckle-edged like expensive invitations. Off the main passage layers of rock doorways and windows like infinitely replicating prosceniums and feints of perspective hinting at rooms hidden behind rooms. She knew that other mapped passages intersected this fenestrated promenade, but as planned she continued on the main route, flying her body, marvelling at rock-lunettes and false oculi in the ceiling. Twenty minutes in, the cave offered a set of curved ribs jutting from the fine silt bottom. Marilyn played her light over the remains. Once upon a time a turtle. Hungry and searching for food or curious and hankering for new sights but either way, run out of air—out of time. Reminder of rock's indifference to the mortal razzmatazz, the sticky particulate, of those trapped in its vast slow yawn. Cave-time, creaturely time—best to keep them straight.

Seventy-five minutes from the start of her descent, she reached her turn pressure, having exhausted a third of her air supply. This left a third for her return and a third for a possible emergency. More-skilled Rand, who slid through the water with greater ease, hadn't breathed down his third yet, despite his greater physical size. But he was accompanying her and so her restrictions governed. What was the body, she thought as they began their exit, but a sad breath-counting machine animated and simultaneously limited by each respiration? Not flying. Never free.

Nearing the entrance again, the backlit mouth of the cave was an azure stain. They spent their brief deco slow-bumping in the water's gentle wash.

Then it was up and out. Leaves glowed like lanterns in the motionless trees.

30

That afternoon they made love in Bowman's trailer. They touched each other carefully as if in touching they could put themselves together piece by piece. Later they drove again to the dive centre and dropped off their doubles for a refill. She grabbed a quick bite to eat from the cooler at the front of the shop which she wolfed in the lot and then they headed in the truck to the same river she'd soaked her foot in the previous night. They entered the basin in wetsuits and, packing single tanks and otherwise far less gear than usual, swam down and entered the large cavern. No need for a line—the entire grotto lit by natural light from the surface. They ascended to the sponge-work ceiling—like a limestone Swiss cheese—and removed their fins, storing them blade-first in a long narrow crack. They pumped their wings full of air—this pinned them to the ceiling. There they pushed onto elbows and knees and wobbled to their feet—upside down as if the ceiling were floor. Or an upside-down ground where their exhaust ponded and, off to one side, streamed the rock wall in silver waterfalls. She and Rand took a seat on a bumpy outcropping. They were like an old couple on a park bench in another world. If they waited here long enough, soon there'd be ducks, kids playing tag, another couple, arm in arm, out for a twilight stroll.

After, she lingered in the basin, lazing among the mullet and gar, face still in and hands grasping the bottom rungs of the ladder to the riverbank. Someone rapped on her head. She broke the surface. Her mask induced a tunnel vision apparent only on land and in that tunnel now was Bowman, munching potato chips. The clack of her reg filled the air and she spit it from her mouth and dunked her chin to clean it of drool. Two raps, knock-knock. Who's there? she grouched.

He threw his head back. Got yourself a live one Petrie, Bowman yowled.

What the fuck? Rand protested a little later. A fucking cavern dive.

Doesn't matter, cowboy. Always do it right. Long hose over and under her shoulder. Not around the tank valve.

Bowman, Rand said.

Bowman kicked at Marilyn's discarded set-up lying on the grass. I mean what kind of total cluster is this? he said. The modified Yugoslavian method? Very. Fucking. Dangerous.

Rand, barefoot and loose-limbed in his board shorts, was grinning like a gorilla in a regular thump-fest. So? he said. Anyone drowns on this shit-box dive would deserve it. Fuck's sake.

She swabbed her arm across her nose to remove any post-dive snot and began unzipping. She might take issue with Rand's choice manner of expressing himself but his larger sentiment she took as a compliment. She might also take issue with Bowman's challenged sense of contemporary geopolitics but she figured a low profile was her best bet with him.

Bowman kept at it though. Whatever you do, princess, don't listen to this guy. He's got you all wrong here. You do what's right and forget about him. Take care of number one.

Fuck you, Rand said, smile dimming.

Am I talking to you? Bowman growled in response without taking his eyes off her. I thought I was addressing the lady.

She turned her back and draped her wetsuit jacket next to Rand's on a nearby picnic bench. Her ears felt plugged and she hopped on one foot and then the other to shake the water free. No way would she allow the old cycle of infections to set in. Not now.

So Marilyn, Bowman went on. Hear you did Slater this morning. Make it to the Ant Tunnel? Or the traverse to Hermann?

She kept her back to them. On the river past the cavern a four-person team prepared to descend Devil's Eye. Male or female impossible to tell in their drysuits and masks and sundry gear.

No, Rand answered for her. Just a little tune-up.

Tune-up? Bowman yelled. Petrie, are you telling me you did a fucking weenie dive?

She turned in time to catch, in quick succession, annoyance, sheepishness, muted determination fleet across Rand's face. She's got some catching up to do, he said.

171

I bet she does, Bowman said. You asshole.

She gaped but Bowman merely crumpled his empty chip bag and dashed a few yards and slam-dunked it in a trash can.

You're hard to like, Rand called after Bowman. You know that?

Bowman moseyed back. Anyway, when're we going to do Cleargate? I can pencil you in for Saturday.

You meaning not Marilyn. She turned away again and grasped the bibbed remainder of her tight suit on either side of her hips and shimmied while pulling down. Her chilled nipples poked from under the thin material of her swim tank. She decided to leave the rest of the wetsuit on for now rather than display her near-naked rump like a baboon in estrus.

Well? Bowman grunted. In or out?

In, Rand said.

She swallowed more nasal drip and suddenly, as if on schedule, felt nauseous. Too much upside-down time. Too much movement too fast. She could hardly keep up with herself. She tilted around and crossed her arms over her chest. Bowman suddenly stared her up and down. Rand stared at the ground. Blackness fringed her vision. Do not, she told herself. Do not even think it.

Cripes, Bowman said. You okay, princess?

What you get for stuffing it beforehand, Rand muttered.

She roused enough to glare. Serious? she muttered.

Uh oh, Bowman cried, flinging up his hands. Let's not have a domestic. At least not in the vicinity of my vicinity.

Her only serious, she told herself, was the river and its cave system. In less than a week she figured she'd be ready for the Eye. As she recalled it, the difficulty was mental compounded by the physical. Her first time in on a now-long-ago training session, she'd shredded the pads on every one of her fingers as she hand-over-handed outcroppings on the Eye's walls, banging herself in against the ripping outflow. After, she could hardly unsuit. Her fingers bled for hours. Before subsequent dives she'd had to bandage each fingertip then wrap it with duct tape. Took a full week for what became clear oozing fluid to stop weeping. She remembered Rand had laughed at her, as had the other cave divers hanging around at the time, Bowman included. So what? The Eye had taken a nip out of her—just a taste of what it could do. What it could do—the canyon-like opening at the bottom of the river led to a soaring rock cathedral inside, a floor like a beach littered with boulder-sized breakdowns in the limestone structure. Past that there was the squeeze of the narrow bedding plane through which she'd grunted and pressed prostrate as a lover against the water-maddened rock. On the other side of the squeeze lay chambers large enough to drive four trains through. The roar of current in her ears had agreed. A channel cut open inside her, a glimmering intuition that felt like a fragment of the geologic dreams of the earth. Inside her, corridors and shining rooms. Territories opening to a largeness bigger than sky.

Bowman and Rand continued to caper and sputter but they'd lost interest in her by now. As they gossiped about people they knew, her gut calmed. The dive team prepping out on the river sank among glittering fish. Like the turtle whose skeleton she'd seen this morning and the massively fat catfish she'd spied on that green-horn dive six years ago—there must have been ten or fifteen of them lolling sumptuously under the scalloped limestone ledges not far inside from the entrance—she and the divers and the fish as did everyone she knew and had ever known belonged to an impoverished history of abbreviation. And yet. Riding the body into inner space felt like leaping beyond all limits. And in light of that knowledge, she didn't care about Bowman or Rand.

A few *holas* rang out and a woman and man strolled toward them. The woman was compact and muscular with confident-seeming strides, the man wiry. Heard you were coming, the woman said and then chinned toward her companion. He's not but I'm flying the Nest on Sunday. Haul down there and do it with me if you want.

Rand scrunched his face and Bowman made as if to swat him. You asshole, Bowman said. Do it. Ask me nice and we'll make it a three-way.

Marilyn ducked her head and shuffled closer to the riverbank. She refused to care. Refused! She had her plan. Put up with the bullshit for now and don't let on. Head in or bust. What Jane did, Marilyn thought. Though she herself had quit once, in Jane's death lay Marilyn's own big chances. She'd take them all the way. Beneath topsoil unlocked by worms and voles and rotting things to underlying rock that yielded to rain. Rain to aquifer in passages that, aerialed on maps, resembled lightning strikes. An aquifer that still existed but soon might not, washed away by rising sea levels. Lost. Like so much else.

Sick again swirled her stomach. She bent over at the river's edge.

31

Over the next several days she entered and re-entered the underworld. Deep and narcotized in Jordan Blue, her blood boomed to the belling curves of grand white walls. She exited with Rand at noon for a first decompression stop at eighty feet. For the sight—seen from the bottom of this tower of water—of trees rimming the top of the sink like eyelashes. For an hour rising in stages through clear liquid like an omphalos between realms. In Torsun Sink she flipped upstream in current that pinged baroquely curlicued rock. Her exit one fast gliss. For that dive's deco, they lounged on their stomachs in the cave mouth, sharing a magazine they'd stowed in a giant baggie that Rand had clipped to the permanent line so they could catch each page's drift before it eddied into the water in schools of ink.

She felt great. Never fucking better. Then less so when, far back in low-flow Milford, rafts of dwarf-sized arches seemed to infinitely recede beyond their lights. This was her fourth day diving the caves. There was the fatigue factor, factor of residual nitrogen. Of cloaked shapes crowding her peripheral vision among the arches, her reg-whine seeming like cave-chant. Mind-fuck was right. She reached her turn-pressure then humped grim and grimmer toward the exit, Rand following behind. Hosts of shadows skittered from her beam. The elation of the last few days dispersed like dingy gas.

But the way in was also the way out. Her slow hour entering meant its torturous opposite. At the thousand-foot-long breakdown field that presaged the end of the dive—a messed-up bedding plane on average three feet, ceiling to floor—she wedged herself stuck repeatedly, raising her head and banging the roof, tanks jammed into nooks and crannies from which she scraped free. She caught her hoses on stubby outcroppings and detached herself by feel. Begging for each dear inch. Begging no rips. No massive air loss. No clawing her fingernails loose. Once or twice Rand's light spasmed from behind. He was near. But in this narrowing, not much help if she needed it. She stopped to lay her head in her forearms. She breathed. That as far as you can go? The question cackled at her. Suddenly the bottom shifted slightly. She put her hand to it—it was warm, pliant as flesh. She felt she could sink through rock, elbow to armpit to chin. As far as she could go. For this.

He was waiting on the leaf-littered ground—he must have passed her during the exit and decommed farther along in the spring basin. She chugged on the surface toward him. Where the water shallowed, she again lost sight of him as she scavenged for solid footing in the muck. She kept her reg clenched in her mouth and her mask on—mostly out of the water, in air now, but not trusting the fact of it. She could easily drown in half a foot of water if she turtled onto her tanks and couldn't flip back. Drown or earn Rand's scorn as he rode to her rescue. Wouldn't he? Scorn her. Rescue her. Finally with a great mud-unsucking she stumbled onto land. A few unsteady steps beneath her hundred-pounds-plus gear and she latched her arms around a tree trunk and twisted her mask from her face. A smoky rosemary scent. Random birds. Smudge of grey sky. He was part-way up the incline now. She zagged for the next nearest trunk. Then on to the next. Like shadows in reverse, various golds glinted off bark and dripping moss. She followed them as far as she could go. Jane, Marilyn kept thinking. Raise you. You crazy bitch.

When she arrived at the truck, he was in the driver's seat, staring straight ahead through the windshield. She waddled to the rear and banged down the door. She wrestled out of her harness and carelessly dropped her tanks and, without breaking down her regs, shoved her rig onto the flatbed then stripped off her suit and suit underwear. She stabbed her legs into jeans and feet into flip-flops. Everything still worked. She yanked a tee on. Made it. Good to go. In the woods a rustling she took for myste-rious. She got in the truck beside him. Ready, he asked, voice flat. What do you think, she snarled.

Sorry, nope. She would not be taking up knitting. Across the chow mein, his expression queered. His scalp gleamed yellow beneath his thinning crew cut more grey than brown now. His knees snicked hers under the table. Wait, he told her. He was only trying to tell her something. He was tired. She was tired. Milford, he argued, wasn't actually complex like Cleargate. If she had trouble with Milford, forget the harder stuff. So there she had it. He'd had it. Sorry, nope.

But come on, she argued, getting her swagger back. Milford was a one-off. Was bullshit. Sor-ry! She flagged the waiter and pointed to her stained beer glass. Sorry, but she had a lot to make up. Ten months' worth of interring herself in her townhouse office while certain others disported themselves in caves and wrecks. She'd give him sorry. But the waiter fast-fetched her beer and she calmed enough to grandly clink Rand's untouched water glass. After dinner—sort-of dinner, as neither of them ate much beyond a bite or two—they rode back to Bowman's in the truck. The tires shirred on the black-silk pavement. There was a crescent-moon pin on the velvet sky. She hoped Bowman would be off shooting cats somewhere, whatever! Who knew how her evening might end?

32

Two non-diving recovery days later she woke shivering and alone in the spare bedroom in Bowman's trailer. She made it to the bathroom for a painful episode then shuffled to the kitchenette and opened the screen door to a humid over-cast. Rand in rumpled boxers was brewing her gas mix. Not good. Good was brewing her own. Proving her responsible worth. She scratched her fingers on the screen to catch his attention and mouth an apology, but if he heard he ignored her. At least Bowman's truck was gone. She scratched her calf. She examined the welts in some nudge of memory which misted until her gut clutched again, which drove her again to the toilet where she listened to a vehicle rustle along the gravel drive and park. She heard voices too low to follow. The kitchen door banged open.

Princess. You, now. Or forever hold your peace.

She bumped along in Rand's truck, mashed between the two men. Bowman chewed gum with gusto and the fruity scent invaded the cab. Outside the truck, moss-draped cypress and pine. A dead armadillo, two. The sun had punched through the overcast and the AC roared. She drew her jacket hood over her head. An hour into the drive, Bowman sharp-elbowed her hip. Still okay, princess? he asked, smacking his gum.

No problems here, boss. That okay with you?

Wise guy. At least you're speaking. Thought you'd gone comatose on us. Thought Petrie here was going to have to pull off the road and I'd be spending my morning CPRing his better half. And that, my friend, would be a piss-off.

Ha, she said.

He parted his lips in an exaggerated smile and wiggled the gum between his front upper and lower teeth before sucking the wad back in his mouth. Just a little conversation, he said.

Not much later Rand cut from the highway for a secondary road through forest and Bowman buzzed down his window and hawked. Sweltering air oozed inside. When the road petered into a rutted dirt path, the truck bounced past abandoned refrigerators and swollen cardboard boxes and lumpy torn trash bags. Rand clung to the wheel and Bowman braced against the door with one arm, the top of the bench seat with the other, which grazed her shoulders. The vegetation thickened into twisting vines over tangled trees and the path became a branch-whipped tunnel. Bowman clicked off his seatbelt and thrust his upper torso out the window, balancing on the sill. Yee-haw, he called and Rand slowed and Bowman drew back inside and sidled sideways so that his back was against the door, his legs heavy on Marilyn's. He knitted his fingers together behind his neck. Now that I've got you two kids here, he said.

Rand jumped the brake, pitching Marilyn and Bowman forward into the dash. You didn't get us fucking lost, did you? Rand said. Get out of this truck and fucking walk, in front of us. You find that fucking site.

Bowman chuckled. Up ahead, he said and resettled in the passenger seat to face forward. I'm just fucking with you. Fuck's sake. You, my friend, are no fun to be around.

The truck rolled again. Dick, Rand said.

Bowman leaned forward and cupped his hands over her ears. Language, he said to Rand. Try to use your nice words. *You* dick.

Rand drove on, double-fisted. Leaves shushed against both sides of the truck and branches niggled like small creatures on the roof. Suddenly Bowman drum-rolled on his knees and cried, Here-here, and the truck lurched to a halt. Cramps seized her and she lunged for the door handle, but Bowman nose-to-nosed her and she cringed back into her seat. Uh-yup, he said lightly.

Looks not in the slightest familiar, Rand said, after a few seconds.

You stupid bastard, Bowman drawled. You were here, what, year and a half ago? With me. And not this one but the other one. And *that* is a long time no see. Meanwhile a whole jungle springs up. Can hardly tell one fucking thing from another. You should fucking know.

Your mouth? Rand said through gritted teeth. Watch it?

Ouchy, Bowman said. You okay, guy? I've been worrying about the princess here. But maybe it's you I should be keeping my eye on.

Then he cracked open the door and slid out. Marilyn made to follow and he caught her. For a second her legs swung uselessly against his as he tamped the ground then planted her firmly. This what you want, princess? he asked. A little fresh air?

She lodged her hands against his chest for balance. She could feel the ridge of muscle beneath the layer of baby fat. Sure boss, she gasped, then rammed into the thicket where she yanked at her pants and crouched. She pressed her lips together to keep from moaning while the stench rose around her.

When she returned to the truck Rand was already suited, rig readied and waiting upright on the truck's gate. Bowman held Rand's harness straps and he hunkered in and adjusted and slogged out of sight. Bowman dragged her doubles and gear box from the back of the truck, then wordlessly scrutinized her preparations before helping her into her harness, his legs straddling hers as he tented open the straps. She let him attach her suit whip to her intake valve over her left breast and gently press it in place. Then he clapped his palms to the side of her face. *You're* the boss, he said, lips close to hers. Don't you forget.

A tremendous drowsiness hazed her head. She should call this one. For real. He hooked his hands under her armpits and guided her to the side of the truck's gate. Sit pretty for a minute, he told her, and busied himself with his own equipment.

Sweat splashed her eyes and black rings floated across her vision but a single thought lit her head. Wait, she said. Did Jane forget?

He snapped his valves and clipped his lights, then steamed full speed into the bracken. Marilyn trundled after him fast as she could without risking a fall.

Bowman bumped up and down in front of her. A tough nut, he called back after a moment, and then he disappeared, as did the path.

She stopped. Jealousy stirred her acid gut now. What couldn't Jane do? Just as suddenly, Marilyn felt ashamed. She wobbled a few steps and clung to a tree then let go to shaky-leg down an incline and finally arrive at the sinkhole's soup of algae and dead leaves. Perhaps twenty feet from the low bank, the men bobbed side by side. Gripping first a tree trunk and then its exposed roots and then sparse tufts of reedy grass, she backed into the basin and paddled out. As if saluting each other, they all three raised their arms to vent the air in their wings— and descended to sixty-five feet where, feeling cooler and far less burdened, she knelt on the coarse bottom. She fiddled with her gages and futzed with the strap attaching her primary computer to her forearm, and on second thought tightened it. She checked her gages again, recalculated her turn-pressure—as an inflowing spring Cleargate required a rule of fourths, not thirds. But then she forgot the new numbers, and then the new-new numbers also thrashed from her brain. She was losing precious time, she knew. But still. Things weren't right and she needed to fix them. Then Bowman rapped her mask. He thrust an okay at her. She tried to gather a quick response but he tried again, and before she could throw an okay back at him he stuck his thumb up. Dive's over. Now she mustered an emphatic O with her thumb and first finger. He shook his head. No. She held his stare until his expression grew more quizzical. He raised his hand horizontally in the water and fluttered it side to side. Something wrong? She shook her head, then gave an exaggerated shrug and pointed first one direction and then another. Which way? Bowman stared another few seconds and then signalled a different direction. There. Where ten feet away, tops, Rand waited and watched.

Cleargate—big and brilliant with white walls nearly a hundred feet floor to ceiling. Their lights blazed. With the inrushing current, she made easy progress. Numerous previously laid lines ran parallel then deviated off the main permanent one through other far-ranging tunnels—one leading to another cave system altogether. Easy for a novice—or someone rusty or otherwise impaired by illness or fatigue or stress or ego—to succumb to a second's inattention and switch off the main line. To fuck up royally and not know until too late to find the way out again. No worries about that here though—locked between Rand and Bowman, she might as well have been diving in a floodlit tin can. Even so she felt uneasy as she surged farther in. Once she called the dive she'd have to slam her way out against the current, more tired than when she began. Not the best scenario. And what was her turn-pressure again? Fear-pressured, she felt her breathing whoosh. She checked and rechecked her gas gage. Twenty minutes, thirty minutes passed. The needle dropping fast, she breathed faster in alarm, and so needed to breathe harder—caught in the vicious cycle of air hunger until, choking, she flailed her light. Bowman near-instantly drew alongside. He touched her shoulder and she snapped her thumb up. Get me the fuck out now. He grasped her, expertly swinging her in the opposite direction. Then he gave her a firm push. Go. For a second, too stunned to respond, she allowed the current to whale her farther back inside. Then Bowman had her again. Another push. Swim, he yelled into his reg. Swim—and she knocked toward the exit and never looked back.

Outside the cave—in the basin, still on the bottom, heaving into her reg—she managed to check her computer. She jerked toward a scramble of sunken tree roots and completed her first stop. Numb. But okay. She ascended for nearly an hour, performing her decoms solo before crawling from the water to haul herself tree to tree to truck where the men were already breaking down their rigs and ignoring her. Fine! Except for some wonkiness in her left arm. Once Bowman and Rand had moved to the front of the pickup to unsuit and swig power drinks from their stash behind the truck's seats, she blammed her tanks down hard on the truck's gate and with difficulty un-velcroed the computer strap from her forearm. She struggled out of her seals and sleeves and gingerly unzipped her underwear and peeled it off. Mother. Fuck. Her left limb was swollen wrist to elbow. No pain yet but she knew what she was looking at— and now she looked back, could picture it all. Stupid. Fussing out of nerves at the bottom of the sink, she'd tightened her computer strap but then in her post-dive numbness she'd forgotten to loosen the strap again before ascending. Should have known better. Below, her suit and underwear compressed slightly but when coming up again they expanded. The tightening strap constricted her circulation. A textbook case. Nitrogen bubbles or even a single glister lodged at a vascular pressure point. This when the cave-like branches and tributaries of her arterial system should have been working as efficiently as possible. Stupid her. Stupid arm. From which she felt curiously unattached. Bent.

33

Only a little, she protested.

No such thing as a little bent, Bowman told her. We'll go down to the chamber in Gainsville, I'll even get in there with you. Those fuckers know me pretty good. You and me, we'll play cards, have a party. You'll be the guest of honour. Now let me take a fucking look.

A TV mounted above the bar blared a fascinating show in which someone might win something, a set of manipulations and negotiations which for a second she couldn't possibly take her eyes off. Then she did. The screen provided illumination for most of the shack, revealing a gray-haired long-hair shucking oysters behind a counter with three empty stools lined against it. She and Bowman occupied some folding chairs at a scratched wooden table that held a saucer of packaged crackers in the middle. Bowman's proposal—lock herself inside a twenty-foot-long steel-drum-like structure while medical personnel re-pressurized the bubble in her bloodstream to re-dissolve and allow it to be safely off-gassed—struck her as pure crap. Lots of people took mild hits and skipped the pony show. Like Bowman never had? Rand? How about tough Jane. Was she right? Marilyn asked, smiling through her teeth.

Fuck, Bowman said and slumped in his chair.

She stopped smiling. What she thought.

Listen, he said without much pep. We eat, we go.

He cut his eyes to the TV then the door. Rand was still outside, reorganizing gear. Also parked in the dusty lot were five motorcycles aslant like giant gleaming insects but with riders nowhere in sight, though they must be some-where inside this plywood-board construction. It must have a hidden addition, an underground space where who knew what went on. One more deception. Her own had been to conceal her condition during the drive here from Cleargate—so far her cover only blown with Bowman, scotched when she'd gone to enter the bar with him and fumbled with the door handle. Now he leaned forward in his seat with apparent new resolve and, latching onto her arm, pulled up her jacket sleeve and squeezed. Still pretty numb. Lymphatic edema, he pronounced.

She reacquired her limb. On second thought, she mounted it awkwardly around his neck and laid her cheek against his collarbone, nuzzled his chin. He tensed but otherwise offered no resistance when she got her lips on his. Then she wiped her mouth with the back of her good hand and said, Thanks. Like I don't know.

Bowman exhaled loudly and refused to look at her. After a moment he slapped the table with his palm. A little help here, he called to the bartender. Three draft, plus three dozen of your finest.

Some prize on the show. Some kind of skill required. Some kind of luck. Applause and smiles. Winner takes all. The shack door opened and Rand stepped out of the nimbus of light, trailing dust motes. Confidentially speaking, a little alcohol'll help, Bowman told her, talking as low and fast as his drawl allowed. Then we'll make room with the gear so you can lie down, and we'll slap some O2 on you. Pump you with codeined aspirin back at the ranch.

Rand seated himself. She avoided his gaze. Hey asshole, Bowman said. Not that I want to break the ice or anything, but a certain little issue has reared its ugly head.

Rand viewed Bowman groggily. What? Rand mimed. So? Bowman plucked her injured limb up and held it aloft. Then with exaggerated care returned it to her. Rand jammed the heel of his hand to his eye. Fuck, he said.

The bartender brought beer and oysters and she stalked to the damp closet-sized bathroom where she tried to relieve herself. Nothing came. She returned to the table, picking and drinking as wordless as Bowman and Rand. All three of them were still under the influence—residual narcosis and adrenaline's wasting dopamine aftermath. Rand looked shrunken, old before his time. Some old geezer too worn to ask how she was doing, if she was okay. Finished with his dozen, Bowman cleared his throat. What's the point, string bean? he said. Maybe you don't care about your own safety. But you might want to think about his.

For a moment she and Bowman observed Rand, who was engrossed in opening a package of crackers.

His? she said, pick-picking again at a shell—she could maneuver with difficulty but still get the job done. He can't speak for himself?

Rand and Bowman both stared straight ahead. More silent treatment! she thought. Was that really such a good idea? She slathered an oyster into her mouth then lobbed the shell onto the plate piled high with empties in the middle of the table. A few shells leapt and skittered onto the floor. Then Rand picked up his fork again and Bowman drank and the bartender removed his shucking glove and mopped his brow with a dishtowel. Soon she let the door slam behind her and, with her good hand, rattled the handle to the truck and scootched in. Sweat ran off her face and sucked between her breasts and soaked her shirt. Hot sharp spikes jabbed her gut. Stomach flu was all she had. Three days of snivelling and god knows and meanwhile her fucked arm would right itself. Deserve or didn't had nothing to do with it. It was just her luck, her fuckhead told her, hammering tight.

PART FIVE

34

No sign of Bowman by the time they hit it northbound. She and Rand stopped only for fuel, fries, other shit he killed on the go while she nursed vitamin waters. Nineteen hours in, a hundred clicks from home, an early snow sparked the night fields beyond a gas station. She managed herself from the truck, Rand sullen at the pump, shoulders hunched to his ears. The thick hose stirred between them. Wind fired their hair. Flakes drifted down.

Pitiful sleep. Now she squinted, stunned by weak sunlight. She parsed the rows of towering red-bricks, their rotting pumpkins on paved paths and polyester ghosts espaliered over shrubs. Orange leaf-stuffed bags. Her home-sweet dime-sized lawn scaly with waste. She shuffled to her front gate holding her arms from her sides as if walking a gangplank, breath in white parachutes. From the mailbox she scooped envelopes and flyers, other peoples' ideas of things, and canted her face sky-ward. Cumuli, starling drift. The cold planed her skin at the jawline and cheekbones. In the hallway again she felt cleansed, de-cored like an apple. Not bad. Her wrist barely ached as she retied the drawstring on her sweatpants. The fabric bunched and she billowed the hem of her shirt over her concave stomach, pelvic bones thrusting like tusks. Last night in bed he'd strummed her ribs—first close contact in a week. You're disappear-ing, he'd said.

Three more recovery days later, smoke jetted from her bony crotch, her ears twirled like whatzits. She hunched over a workbench in the garage and squeezed a tube of silicon, wanding the applicator over crushed neo-prene. Never mind the slices in her drysuit's kneepads, her mind eeled along—never mind a week ago she'd rocketed from Cleargate terrified beyond her skull and before that crawled a thousand feet through Milford's mandibles of flooded rock, mask a bedazzle of tears, claustrophobia banging her brain. Never mind—here was the situation. On those dives she'd silently begged for mercy, but she'd done a fair job calculating her gas usage, a more than fair job embracing the biochemical curtsies and swoons and soaring exchanges in the blood-stream that had her at addict, at more—she whistled a mechanical seesaw while she worked now, just thinking. Next dive—deeper, if she planned it right. If all went according to plan. And when the inner garage door slung open—her husband just home from the office, wincing, last night's congress evidently forgotten—she stored her suit on a hanger and recalled how much the custom fit cost back in the day. Now she'd have to get it taken in. Restore the dark shape to her own newer, trimmer one. How much that would cost her.

As if he were thinking the same thing, the pinched face on him. As if he should care! She let fly and cornered him by the tanks. Shirt wilted and trousers creased around the groin. He puffed his cheeks and extended his neck at an angle usually seen on men too old to fix. Where were his glorious blue tats now? Gone, erased like stubborn but not invincible water marks. Do not threaten me, he said. He said, Everything is different now. Game changed. You're different now.

Huh, she said. Is that right?

He kept working his jaw. Finally his voice seemed to catch up with the motion and he said, I'm trying to make this simple so you can understand. I am not babysitting you anymore. No. More. Get it?

Well now, she said, and twitched her chin with her thumb to pantomime thinking. She said, For a man of few words you suddenly have a lot to say. She said, Threaten? Don't mind if I do.

35

The next morning Bowman said, Princess, don't make me get on the blower with him.

She said, Try it, baller. I think there's something you're forgetting. She said, What? I tell you I'm going to dive Marshall Wall deep on air, no fancy gas mixes. And what? You think I should solo it instead?

A little later she slammed her car door. Rand had already left for the day but Bowman she couldn't seem to lick—he was in her earpiece like cream in a Twinkie. Dickweed. Why she ever had to kiss him. Ugly did not begin to say. So she shut it and cranked the heat, then trammelled right then left and ran a yellow. Smile for the camera. Cool and bright today. Bowman croaked on— another story. She transponded the newest limits with their upstart municipal checkpoints gussied folksy— single-story cinder blocks with polyurethane-thatched roofs and guards in belled floral skirts and dimity slacks and purple-laced jackboots. When had all that happened? She roared past pillared entrances to the interconnected subterranean malls and finally coasted the old residential streets once wide as fields and now as doll-tiny as the old Jane and old Marilyn—such girls. She nosed the car by a life-sized woman wrestling some recycling curbside. Two boys sworded sticks across a narrow lawn. In Marilyn's rearview they vaulted the narrow ditch and clambered into the road to remonstrate in her direction like miniature trolls. She cruised the main thoroughfare, every second or third bronzed doorway a restaurant or specialty market with storefront windows boasting signs in Cyrillic and Korean, Farsi and Franglish—as far as she could tell all saying You Should Eat. Her stomach rumbled. Resolute, she toured alongside the park she and Jane, once upon a time, practically owned—it appeared strangely unchanged save for being uninhabited. She buzzed down her window and stuck out her head, single-handing the wheel. Swings swung in the lilting wind. Sugar maples rustled their last few crimsons and umbers. Princess? Bowman said. Still there?

Still there. Here, barely. She pulled over. Sparrow, grass. She'd fallen behind. Her adipose cross-sections and abnormal thyroids modelled in cinereous hand-drawn pencil sketches, then software-remodelled—her bread and butter—lay half done and not done. Undone—ten days off for a little vacay south with the husband and all goes to hell? So much for her ancient history of steady-Freddy building relationships with clients. So much for all that, she thought as the engine ran and ran until she thought to cut it. She circled her wrist in the air, testing. Bowman continued to carp, nearly bleeding her auricles. Bad idea, he kept saying. Rand is right, princess, that is one bad idea. You do not need to do that fucking dive now. Or ever. You have everything to lose. You. Him. You hear me?

She heard him. She knew. But she also thought, yes, but you've had your bad ideas. And survived them.

And this idea, she thought, is mine.

And losing? Don't even get her started. For starters, she'd already lost and lost. And how could Rand know what it felt like to really lose someone? She remembered thinking this clearly for the first time maybe six months into their marriage. Came out of nowhere, felt like. They were in the kitchen and there was the broken bowl. Her mother's. What was Rand's grief—what were his griefs—by comparison? Adopted as a baby, he'd never known his parents. When she first met him he was already half a lifetime into surely a lesser state of grief than hers. How could he love what he'd never really had? He broke the bowl—an accident, apparently, always accidents—and she leaned her hip against the dishwasher and took in the blue shards on the maple floor. How could he? The broken bowl, his dim fucktard apology. Or whatever he was calling it. Sorry!

In her car now she gripped her fingers around the wheel. Anger and pain jaundiced every chamber of her heart. Instead of the park with its swing set and fiery maples, she saw three people who together had hooked and crooked a big mess. Her mind flooded, just thinking. She licked her lips and buzzed up her window and peered through the windshield, longings fulvous as the rotting leaf piles that reminded her of sepsis and the mephitic whiff of sewers and sulfurous sinkholes to which she felt astonishingly drawn. Where Jane went. Where Marilyn now understood she might still go. How astounded she suddenly was by herself. In her wildest dreams in her old life of work and work, she would never have thought that who she was now was possible. That she could possibly think, Stupid crier, at Bowman's yacking and clacking Hear Ye's. That she could be this bored up here in the boring bounded world, a portly squirrel lugging a bagel beneath a red-and-blue teeter-totter, four black helicopters as usual fleeting the west as smoke plumed one or two mercantile citadels, evidence of incendiaries and injunctions and nothing and everything to do with her and hers. Business as usual on a day so ordinary she could puke, she pressed End Call.

She parked at the cemetery. *Pardes Shalom.* The car's heater blasted. She undid her coat, hiked her dress to her hips and waited for Bowman's callback. She traced the pattern on her thick tights as if memorizing the peaceful garden's snaking ridges—as if her tight's woven tattoo echoed the rows along the hill before her, lanes organized by affiliations and denominations here distributed under crusting and crimping sycamores and stalwart evergreens skirting the spiny arrays of east-facing headstones, including her parents' double memorial.

Soon though she tired of waiting—heart hot and heavy, lickety-splickety she dug in the bucket placed next to the path. Despite the pain in her forearm.

Because of it. And in no time she had rocks in her coat pockets and hands. Rocks dun-coloured and heather grey flecked with quartzite. Rocks smooth and flat and round and rocks shaped like stars, plums, dates. The pretty pit of Bowman's Adam's apple—how it jumped when she'd rammed her tongue between his teeth to quiet him at the corner table in the oyster shack. Narcotized and stupid-novice bent, or merely assailed by some stomach bug, Bowman's slutty drawl edging into her and then, hours later, back at Bowman's, she couldn't unload her gear from the truck. Rand's silence a bludgeon. Bowman a shadow evanescing altogether. What was he, scared? Pussy. What was she? Monster, going and going. That night he'd stayed gone and the next morning too and then she and Rand left. Six days no calls and now? Rand must have gabbed on her.

She stood with her rocks. She knew! Losing. It's what she did best. It occurred to her she could lose whatever it took.

To clear things out, tunnel to the root, whatever. Get at this new-new thing she'd never seen before. Her. Herself.

Up the hill she now went. Above the trees an undammed sky so blue her veins hurt. Her eyes hurt—her fovea pricked by tiny dots. She cuddled into her coat. The lumps in her pockets bruised her legs. Rocks in her head, she traversed the swale and arrived at ma and pa in no time and laid her offerings to rest. How parched she was. Dying.

36

Forget the soured sun on Bowman's flimsy trailer and oyster shacks not exactly booming with business. This far north—way past the most weakly guarded perimeter—and this late in the season most of the peninsular town's shop and hotel windows were boarded up in anticipation of a harsher-than-last winter's harsh. Many of the cottages that cusped the lake side and semi-circled the bay side and serried through the wooded hills most likely already had their pipes shut. Rand drove fast, scudding the gravel while, visible through chinks in pine forest and sumac, white-capped waves reared. Soon Rand parked his black behemoth behind Leo's white one, next to the timbered A-frame set back from the road in a stand of cedar and spruce. When Marilyn thumped on the front door, faded leaves drifted against her ankles and pine needles matted under her feet. No answer. Her stomach cramped and her head swam. Suddenly she could hardly believe she was here, about to go through with things. And, leaning against the door frame to steady herself, she could hardly believe she wouldn't. Which fear was worse?

You told him four, right? Rand groused from the truck—one more thing for her to manage. He blurred then snapped into focus, frowning and hoisting a backpack.

She knocked again then turned the handle and let herself in. Mildew and acrid cleanser. She mounted the three stairs from the vestibule into the living room. A hushed movement mounded under a plaid throw on the couch and she slowly backed out. On the drive again, wind spattered grit and her lungs burned. But Rand had dumped their overnight bags on the ground and was rummaging behind the truck's cab and she felt she should hurry and help, except she felt like balloons let go.

Call it, she told herself reasonably enough, but once started on that track she found she couldn't stop. Call it, she thought, and forget living to tell the tale. Forget living. Without the diving, even if it meant near-dying, how would she know she was alive? And not back in the past with her dead. Dead herself.

Marilyn? Rand said loudly, sounding agitated. You want all this food shit inside too?

Don't say it, she told herself. Do not say, How weird is this? Guess we better head on home. Don't say, Sorry Rand. Putting you through all this trouble. What was I thinking? You're right, guess I wasn't.

She closed her eyes for a second and imagined his sneer. His, I'll bet you're sorry.

She strode forth and yanked the grocery bags from him. A slight twinge from her wrist but otherwise it seemed fine. Yes, Rand, she said firmly. I want it all.

He refused to budge as she edged past him and plunked the bags on the front passenger seat of the truck. She rummaged behind the truck's cab for the beer stash. Hey, Rand said. You helping or not?

Leo, she said. That asshole. He's upstairs getting off. Can you believe? Let's crack a couple right here and wait a few. Pretend everything's normal. We know how to do that, right?

No problems here—within the hour Rand and Leo were on the patio with the rusty outdoor grill fired up and she was in the kitchen opening a bag of fancy salad and scouring the cupboards and drawers for evidence of utensils and plates. In the fridge she located gelatinous bottled dressing. She sipped another brew and finally counted out three paper-and-plastic place settings—Leo's probable paramour having apparently evaporated through the rear door. But mostly she considered tomorrow's forecast. Possible thunderstorms. Ripping winds. She could hear the wind now, netting the occasional flash of the guy's laughs. If Leo could get them out on his boat to the dive site tomorrow she'd have to really have her shit tight. No screw-ups on the roistering deck, in the mashing confusion mistakenly placing one piece of gear where another should go. No puking over the gunwales. No getting dehydrated-weak—asking for another hit, her already-damaged tissues unable to conduct nitrogen as effectively as healthy ones. How many more chances could she take? She'd been deep on air before, lots of times, had the self-mastery thing down, but never in such harsh conditions. Never managed herself so much, so deep. Now was her chance. She could check it off her list. She had her plan. Let no one—not Rand who she had over a barrel, not Bowman, not even herself—get in her way. She held her bottle up to the kitchen light. Half empty. She gurgled the rest down the sink and, straightening her back, winched herself tall.

The gusts kept up all through dinner which she only picked at and soon their florid rushes accompanied the movie she and Rand and Leo watched, one they'd all seen before. Leo periodically checked the marine forecast. When she and Rand retired early to the guest lair, she fell asleep immediately, an errant airstream hooking her ankles and hauling her upside down and far away, hair trailing below, the wind jubilant, black, if black were a sound.

She woke to find her husband practically on top of her. Mare, you awake?

She opened to him and he entered and fucked her. She was about to come when, from Leo's bedroom next door, she heard above her own wail another woman's. Marilyn grew rigid. Stretching his mouth over hers, Rand ground away, beating a succession of cries from her which passed into him.

Blown out, she and Rand and Leo played cards all the next morning. Still no sign of Leo's mystery crush. At one point he scrambled some eggs and they ate. They watched more movies and slept again. Mid-afternoon she got up and washed her face then took a walk. A brute raw day. By the side of the road, the trees shorn of leaves scraped and bent and threw up their bows as if pissed. From here, half a forested mile inland, she failed to see the vast tract of water. And yet the enormous bay on one side joining with the great lake on the other filled her mind. Their increasing poisons, given the damaged world. This open water. No entering a cave or a wreck on this dive. No inside unfolding as if into a labyrinthine infinitude. Instead, a seemingly formless gray-blue blotting and snuffling the shore. And yet not open, not formless. A scaffolding of levels—each with its own exigencies depending on depth and temperature and light and viz. Each level of a deep open-water dive demanded a plan like an airy set of trusses delicately cantilevered over liquid in an architecture invisible to the naked eye. So she'd planned. All her plans, she thought now. What of them? She'd plotted and schemed to superintend what she could of her parents' skittery presence. Jane's too. Even Marilyn's own breaking marriage. As if that would keep them all safe, herself included. Safe from herself.

This wind. Leo's boat wouldn't have a chance against the insane surface conditions. Tomorrow would likely be a wash. As if in response the sky began to hiss and spit. She marched anyway, past the locked cottages lining the road like blocks in a wall, trooping like a rat on a treadmill. Inside her, a juiced-wire lashing. On and on she went, ghosting everyone she knew and had ever known. Refused to know. Her mind a fastened hatch.

She returned to the cottage to find Rand alone in the living room, dark except for the TV. She turned the lamps on for him as one might for an invalid. Leo had left for the shop where he was tying up business odds and ends. After this weekend he'd close for good for the season. Around four in the afternoon she and Rand made sandwiches with the bread and cold cuts they'd brought. They read old dive magazines and spy novels plucked from the rickety bedroom shelves. Leo called at six.

Bag it, Rand said over the phone and she clicked the off button on the TV remote. No glory in losing your boat, he said after a moment had passed, then he fingered his scarred temples and listened some more. Fuck's sake, he continued. *I* can do it.

He hung up and tossed his device onto the couch beside him, refusing to meet her gaze.

She said, Thanks for the sterling recommendation, boss.

He rose. Piss off, he said and stalked from the room and down the stairs.

The front door slammed. She took a shower and dressed again then lay down in her clothes and scored another nap. She woke at eight o'clock at night. She stared at the darkened ceiling. Soon it was nine. The TV kettle-drummed and keened from the living room. She trudged to the bathroom. In front of the mirror she untangled her hair and harped a fingernail along the ridges of her comb. Puh-link puh-lunk. At ten Leo called again to report the wind was down.

She and Rand climbed in the truck. He backed onto the road, bumpety-bump. Drive faster, she nearly said, but already he was picking up speed as he rounded the first corner. The road was so dark she wished he'd turn off the headlights. See what happened next.

37

So stoned.

As if in a glass jar, suspended among drifts of white gauze. She was diving relatively deep, breathing air just to feel the effects and here they were. Metallic pings and sonorous snores—her breath a miracle-soup. She halted her descent and studied the display on her primary computer. Instantly the fog around her brightened—hello synapses roaring back into business. She swept her beam through the tar-waters below. The jagged monochrome contours of the limestone cliff revealed themselves. Forty-foot viz, she guessed. She guessed she better recheck her computer and gas gages. Another recheck to let the situation really sink in—two hundred and five feet. Noted. Also, she was shaking with cold though she felt lit as a drunk jacketless on a frigid night. She picked her way lower, avoiding the sludge-furred rock. Stir that and she'd reduce her light to a hazy circle swallowed by silt. Check and recheck. Two-fifteen. Two-twenty-five. Her breath was an accordion wooze. Noted—at this depth the slightest spike in her inhalations would at the very least enhance the narcosis. Noted—breathing harder could also spike the oxygen levels in her bloodstream to toxic levels. She'd convulse, drown. Noted—the need to check and recheck, work the sloppy cantering horse of her brain and understand the slipshod bullshit she was in.

Plus she'd lost sight of Rand.

She directed her beam toward her chest. Darkness exploded. She gazed further down the inky well and picked out the faint gleam of a beacon fading fast. Thirty feet below her? Rand, breathing air at the limits of where air should be breathed—and here her mind dismounted. Not here. In white veils trailing hidden streams, where a gondola floated beneath crumbling aqueducts, a barrel-chested boar sang, striped boater at a rakish angle. From a nearby tavern thrilled a wolf-whistle coloratura. She disembarked here and entered through a thick oak door. A colony of grey cats with cricket tongues greeted her, chirping notes like chipped tesserae in an ancient mosaic. She tried to swallow but her throat was a dry bone no drink could help. What could? Hurry, she thought.

She again cast her light. The aureate slope was like an old painting fading around its edges. She stroked her beam up and down. Urgent. Please respond. Zip.

Options, please.

Please?

She could still figure that Leo was somewhere above. She'd last seen him bailing on his dive in the vicinity of

210

a hundred-seventy feet. The boat meanwhile had been left unattended, an illegal move in any book—no one to make sure the anchor didn't break free, no one to prevent the former fishing tug from surging away and capsizing, from colliding with other night-plying vessels. No one on board to radio for help in case of an emergency. No one left. No help.

Rand's light expired.

She gorged, fattened on fog. Blood sirened through her veins. Her heartbeats a sortie of hobgoblins. Down she went after him. Two-thirty, god-forty. Special delivery. She no longer shivered in her golden cocoon. No longer anything but a delivering machine.

She called it at two-fifty-seven. She felt the decision as physical, neural-glandular, pineal as a third eye. Pure primitive. She turned and faced the broken slope and commenced her ascent. It took forever. She saw it could be her unstinting present, that it pre-existed her, like a mold she would pour herself into for the rest of her life. So she would live after all. Some weepie. As she went she periodically scanned behind. No sign. Her head slowly cleared but she mostly ignored it though she continued to understand the need to attend her gages, her pace. She noted a tickle in her left eye. It hung in her sight like a sac of hope and she cursed it. Why hope now? She shuddered, clinging for a moment to the rock face, and then relief hatched in her belly and swarmed her chest.

She waited. Eventually Rand passed her with no notice and she climbed again until, somewhere in his vicinity, she made her first decompression stop for a minute at a hundred feet. She continued trailing, switching to her decom gases from extra tanks slung at her sides. By the time she reached thirty feet she and Rand hung together in a balmy fifty degrees, having risen through several thermoclines. She had to pee. Otherwise with little sense of urgency she prayed that the boat and Leo waited on the surface to ferry them back. That they'd all gotten away with something.

At twenty feet she and Rand rested against a massive limestone outcropping riddled with holes the size of quarters. Hang time, major deco. They turned off their beams to conserve the batteries and lay in darkness to avoid attracting swarms of the underwater life that existed at these warmer, shallower depths, the tiny pale freshwater shrimps and nits that already fashioned a twittering corona around her and Rand—the two of them larger bugs sparking in a dark field. Occasionally they plied a small backup light and checked their instruments and when they did the illuminated limestone became a crayfish condo—at each of the thousand windows, antennae pricked, the crustaceans waved at visitors once giants but now nearly fish food. How close they'd come.

PART SIX

38

She woke drenched and threw off the spread.

Bright spring flowed in the open window—finally. Spring, or something like it.

Cooling, she again closed her eyes. She'd committed some terrible crime. Awaiting incarceration, she received her dead mother—dead but an uncancered whole again—in the living room of their old home. The old family sheepdog there too. Time for new goodbyes. Marilyn had never felt so loved! Then the appointed hour neared. She entered a narrow sunken street of ancient cobblestones and darkened shops. Lost and alone she paced and retraced her steps in a cold rain. Soon a white delivery van slid alongside, windows streaked. She got in the back seat. Noted with gratitude the heater blasting—she'd never felt so cold. The driver turned toward her. Rand, his face dirt-streaked as raw beets. Eyes slitted against her. She wondered how long he'd been crying.

She woke again, foggy, and plumped the pillows and sat and soon the dream-dross melted. Like this past winter—always the snow like tiny cold seeds, and then hyacinths in the neighbours' terracotta pots. Ivy slickening green and ascending the walls of her towering tower of a house. Outside the bedroom window, three stories down, children's pipsqueak voices bouncing like white balls. Did not, did so. Did so. As the children passed by, their voices trailed off, like dots of light elongated with dark tails.

On another morning not much later, first of a long weekend—nearly summer again, nearly a year since Jane's death—Marilyn woke at dawn to a silver light like none at all. She woke her husband and they readied and then she drove, cutting east-north-east past the latest checkpoints and then through the rolling hills. They stopped for grilled cheeses they barely ate and made a night of it in a motel where they turned to each other briefly, then turned away—Rand with a bad cough. Nothing really, he insisted, though it bore holes and tunnels in their sex and sleep and ended as leaks in memory-murmurs of things passed—Jane's teeth picking around the pit of a plum and Bowman rasping of princesses and weenies. Reminding Marilyn when she fully woke at five the next morning—of what? Remind her? Bowman for-real dead this past winter deep in a cenote in Tulum. Turned into one more storied frog, croaking prince for some princess. And so, some seven months after she'd kissed Bowman, frogs in his honour heaped from a snoring Rand's ears onto the motel bed and laurelled her with chorus-croak. They drowned the sad roar in her head and then drowned her back to sleep again.

Late again, very late. They suited up at high noon on the low bank of the northern river. Cold. Strong current out there. The water green, grey, green, depending. Rand opened a valve on his doubles and a hose ripped. He cursed and hacked and spat. She pulled her hood over her head and filled that with the tender leaves on the trees backing the riverbank. Then she swapped those leaves for the weeping willows of her childhood. They'd once thrived on the banks of the old neighbourhood creek that snuck under roads and culverts and rose snaking through parks and the alleys behind people's homes. She and Jane smoked not only their first cigarettes but also their first joints by the creek slope while sleek muskrat sunned, doubling in the water's mirroring sheen. Marilyn's first period commenced there and, two days later, so did Jane's. The creek long ago filled in by bulldozers and the willows replaced by invasive survive-at-all-costers—honey locust and ailanthus, tree of heaven. Here it was mostly spruce and scrappy maples and birch not fully budded out yet but she wondered at briefly feeling the old wonderment and soon Rand's foul curses subsided. He finished changing over his hose. Shadows flitted among the branches and shades of branches impossible to distinguish for real. Especially given the distraction of his grunting and coughing. His increasingly gaunt frame. Postpone? she asked him on the days leading up to this trip, and he'd shrugged her off and she'd let him. It's on, was all he'd say.

Was it? she thought. Still? Last fall seemed to her like a burst blister. She felt less on and more out—of grief. Fresh out. And when he coughed and glanced at her now from the rear of the pickup and grimaced—or smiled, who knew?—she wondered why he wanted to do this dive today. Why she did. They just did. Her own thoughts felt like afterthoughts, accidental the way Jane's death was ruled an accidental drowning. She'd knocked her tank manifold hard enough in some tight crevice that she lost all her air at once. Never had a chance.

Your turn, he said, his face now the ordinary face of a tired ordinary-looking pock-faced man—it surprised her that he was someone she knew. He donned his mask and maneuvered his flashlight-rigged helmet onto his head and fastened the chinstrap. Over his neoprene gloves he pulled a pair of lightweight mesh Kevlar ones, like hers, designed to protect hands when scaling and gutting fish—handy for feeling through the razor-edged limestone in today's cave. He shouldered his rig and affixed his extra tanks to his sides and laboured by.

She clapped on her helmet and weaselled into her harness and snagged her stage bottles then hurried to catch up. She hadn't dived this cave in ages, but he had more recently—with Jane—and so knew exactly where to find the submerged entrance near the river's far shore, overgrown with impassable bracken. But once he showed Marilyn the mouth, she'd be on her own. They'd both agreed. Having studied the map, fruit of his and Jane's careful surveys, Marilyn knew what to expect. No more trust-mes.

*

She waddled into the shallows. A kingfisher buzzed the low bank and crows pecked pebbles beneath him. Rand was already waist deep and bent over in the swift current, doubles riding huge on his back, stage bottles like torpedoes under his arm. He horked—a protracted gargling sound. Fuck, he yelled. Fuck, I'm strangling—and she removed the reg from her mouth and called, Wait, her voice rusty, but he gave a push toward the middle of the river and dropped from view. Bubbles from his breath-exhaust flurried on the surface for a second or two until the racing water annealed any evidence of him. She waded further in. Her ears whistled and popped and she felt thirsty as crestlets curled around her calves. She wanted to drink then shed her gear and sleep tight as an egg high out of the river, but what would she do with herself then? She passed deeper still into the river until she could no longer touch bottom, then she vented her wings and banged to the river's floor where she hauled hand over hand along the rocks, mindful of the surge that might sweep her miles downstream. The tips of his fins emerged and disappeared from time to time. Finally she came upon him, a curiously again-hulking figure, wreathed in a clump of streaming water-weeds. Okay? Okay. Rock-rubble and bloated forest debris materialized in the gloom. He tied off to a log and turned on his main light. Then he disappeared limb by limb through a narrow slit at the base of the pile.

A rise, a fall. Dark and then bright. Inside, water so clear. And a violence of esses and zees and blade-sharp rock-shelves. False ingresses, she knew from having memorized the map. Fly-trap tunnels suddenly closing thirty feet or so in. Time wasters, potential victimizers depending on how stuck one got—but here, tied to his line-reel-line, was the permanent one he and Jane had reliably placed low along the middle of the main passage. For now, Rand himself nowhere in sight. He'd already moved on ahead.

She dragged herself in against the heavy outflow. Decent viz—rough gravel and coarse sand comprised the cave floor, a layer that settled quickly when disturbed. She arrived at the first of his staging tanks and hooked hers next to his. She passed a tee—another line, which veered into a decent-sized secondary passage. Past this, she passed his second-stage bottle, where she dropped hers. Then another tee slipped into view. Her lungs concussed and her head drummed in the current and now and then, when she stopped to check her gages, the current waved her back ten, twelve feet. Still she kept on, in and in. She drew alongside a young sturgeon, roughly three of its potential six adult feet. It lay wan and motionless on the bottom. Fearful, certain the eyes would be nibbled on and the anus and guts deconstructed—sucked how much she could just see it! the body loosening, breaking up—but unable to resist the temptation, she reached her hand to the creature's bony plates, a design unaltered, aside from death's untidying ministrations, since the Upper Cretaceous. No change for some, she thought. At her touch the fish twitched its barbels and roused sluggishly, only to resettle a few feet away. So sorry! her brain sang. Sorry to disturb.

On and on! At some point she'd cross paths with her husband but for now she enjoyed her own pace. Despite

the current she felt unencumbered, a thing that coun-
terbalanced the water pressing out—her own force
an equal pressing. And so on, and when an hour and
change passed, at a depth of fifty-one feet, she reached
the wall collapse that marked the end of the line. Made
it. Time to turn.

But somehow she'd missed him—and suddenly felt
as if she'd swallowed some of the gravel bottom. She
clutched an outcropping of sharp rock to steady herself.
She reasoned that he must have taken one of the teed
lines. Except she hadn't noticed a marker at either line
junction to indicate he'd done so, in accordance with
safety protocols.

She waited for him to show. Shit, shit. Every dark
scudding thing flew in her head.

And then there he was in front of her, or behind,
depending. He seemed suddenly enormous, too large
for the rock to hold him. Or for her to slip by. A parox-
ysm of sound exploded from his regulator, as if he were
spewing crab shells, and he thrust his small underwater
writing slate at her—identical to the one she carried,
grease pencil attached, in a small pouch on her harness
waist. The words took her long seconds to make out.

> YOU ARE TO
> FUCKING SLOW
> TO EXIT

She clapped a hand to her own regulator. The ceiling
lurched closer. The thought of water stuffed her nose

and she felt as if the numbers on her gages might twirl and caper. Heat surged through her torso. He plucked the board from her and swiftly shifted his new-bulk around and, rearing his fins at her, vanished with a stroke.

She mounted the current and set out. On and on, on her own she soared above the permanent line as if it were string to her kite. Once, she skidded past a cork-screw corner and somersaulted before righting herself and then with care threaded her way as if through the eye of a needle. Twice at least she told herself that more than an hour in equalled half that to auger out. She told herself she could do it. Because! her head sang. Because the swift outflow, and because time passed—it must—it seemed to take no time to recover her staged tanks and pass the tees. No markers, as before. No Rand. Still in? Or out? Near the cave entrance where the perma-nent line ended or began—depending—she called it. Because, because. She unfastened his reel and rewound its thread into open water. On her knees on the river bottom, shuddered by current, for a moment she bowed her head. Then she clipped his reel to her harness and hustled forward, crossing toward yet another shore, heart chunking behind like discarded bait. She won-dered who she'd be when she got there.

Acknowledgements

Thanks to Jackie Kaiser, and to Emily Donaldson and the rest of Biblioasis. A special, endless thanks to John Metcalf. Thanks also to Xu Xi. Thanks to the editors of the following journals, who first published excerpts, in different forms: *Sententia, Joyland: A Hub for Fiction, Blackbird*.

As always, thanks to my family and friends for their support. And to David Smooke: for everything.